An American in Heaven

First published by O Books, 2009
O Books is an imprint of John Hunt Publishing Ltd., The Bothy, Deershot Lodge, Park Lane, Ropley, Hants, SO24 0BE, UK
office1@o-books.net
www.o-books.net

Distribution in:

UK and Europe
Orca Book Services
orders@orcabookservices.co.uk
Tel: 01202 665432 Fax: 01202 666219
Int. code (44)

USA and Canada
NBN
custserv@nbnbooks.com
Tel: 1 800 462 6420 Fax: 1 800 338 4550

Australia and New Zealand
Brumby Books
sales@brumbybooks.com.au
Tel: 61 3 9761 5535 Fax: 61 3 9761 7095

Far East (offices in Singapore, Thailand, Hong Kong, Taiwan)
Pansing Distribution Pte Ltd
kemal@pansing.com
Tel: 65 6319 9939 Fax: 65 6462 5761

South Africa
Alternative Books
altbook@peterhyde.co.za
Tel: 021 555 4027 Fax: 021 447 1430

Design: Stuart Davies

ISBN: 978 1 84694 230 3

A CIP catalogue record for this book is available from the British Library.

Printed by Digital Book Print

An American in Heaven

Gordon Phinn

BOOKS

Winchester, UK
Washington, USA

CONTENTS

1	On with the Show	1
2	Back at the Dorm	4
3	Sweat	6
4	Amy Walks In	11
5	The State I'm In Now	16
6	Bummers	27
7	The Victim's Island	35
8	God Hides	44
9	More Family Crap	51
10	Some Fun Stuff	58
11	Wanna Tell Ya	65
12	My Useless Brothers	76
13	The Afterlife Gloomies	83
14	Another Time on the Island	90
15	My Residence	95
16	Nighttime on Earth	102
17	Things Happen	111
18	The End of Avoidance	122
19	The Following Chapter	132
20	Reading the Newspaper	137
21	Pastor Liz	146
22	Something Different	151
23	More of the Same	161
24	What It All Means	167
25	What About Andrea?	184

1. On with the Show

You know that denial thing that everyone accuses everyone else of being in, sometimes to their face and sometimes behind their back, well I've just finished with mine – finished for good. Let's face it; I'm dead – as dead as any ghost or gothgirl with a slash job. As dead as any way you've got of defining it. Oh, you can hide in the endless fun all you want, burrow in like some kitten under blankets, and be as comfy and cozy as you'd ever want to be, but eventually you gotta fess up and see it: you and everyone around you is dead, and this place – whatever it actually is – is Happydeadland on heavy rotation.

By this point I'd been in town for ages, drifting from party to party whenever, you know, and sleeping it off wherever I saw a couch that looked soft and empty. Even empty was negotiable. Just like the old days really, just minus the parents and the job. No limiting yourself to weekends here. What's a weekend? Sixty hours of life between two stretches in the slammer. No slammers here, natch, except maybe the ones you make for yourself.

There's something about fun that makes me wanna slap on a suit and tie and shout from the rooftops. Shout about freedom and fun and be listened to. Suits and ties are always listened to. Teen girls in tank tops and tight jeans never are. It's like we got nothing to say. Well, we got lots to say. Least I did. I'm nineteen not nine, you know?

Motor mouth Melinda: that was grade nine. Major Mel: that was grade twelve. Even Dad called me that, when he called me anything. But enough of this character establishing crap. You'll get that as we go along, if that's what you want. On with the show.

I hadn't been hanging with anyone special. You don't really have to do that here, though you get plenty of offers. Boys missing their mothers if you ask me. But what do I know I'm just a teen girl in tight jeans, right? I don't know any of that Freudian shit, never did get to college. But I did have an English teacher who told me my work was very Freudian. My psycho stories I called 'em; very goth and gloomymoody; Edgar Allen Pop-Goes-The-Weasel; heroines in black capes and diapers; plots of dastardly contrivance; boring as shit.

Like I say, I hadn't been hanging with anyone special, just a couple of guys off the tit long enough to know they really missed it. Quite manageable as long as they know a little suck's comin' up soon. Always been one for offering the boob; found out early on its pacification potential. And here you can manufacture your own milk in a flash. Amazing shit really.

Anyway, parties, dance clubs, concerts, hangin' out, getting' it on, getting' it off and getting' it together. The cool rehearsal for the even cooler performance, and I'm perfecting that one, I can tell you. All those girl-nerves are gone. Well, just about. I can do Marlene Dietrich at the Blue Angel, or Audrey Hepburn at Tiffany's, Ingrid Bergman in Casablanca, not to mention that whole Annie Hall shtick. Used to be the costumes were a pain, but here, well, you just plan it out in your mind and, bingo, it's there. *And* you can do the cigarette thing without the cancer problem.

Born actress that girl, my mother used to say. Kinda envious I always thought. Bit too strait-laced for her own good: got her a husband with a career and shit, but what else? Such a boring life. But the trouble with basket cases, I've decided, is you can't tell them anything. They've lined that basket with their kind of goodies, so to them it feels like a picnic, the whole shebang. They can't see they're stuck in that basket – least my mother can't; never could; still can't. I come to her, in the bedroom at night, and she's like so happy to see me – all huggy and weepy – and we go through the whole dead daughter routine, and I say *Mom we went through this the last time, the last ten times, I gotta new life, it's fine, it's really fine*. And she just smiles and weeps some more. I tell her it's her, that she's gotta get a life, not me, I'm doing great. And she looks at me, like you know, my little girl all grown up and I just wanna puke. Who's the girl here? Really.

During the day, when I'm not too busy myself, which isn't often, I come by and watch her messing about the house, making work after all the work is done, throwing shit on the floor so she'll have to pick it up again, washing the *phones* for God's sake, all until my brothers get home from school. I stand with my hands on my hips and shout at her, just like she usta do to me, but she doesn't hear. They never can, no matter how loud you go. I even slapped her a coupla times, that was kinda cool, but she just rubbed her cheek like she was itchy, and went on with the dusting.

Other times, I'll catch her with the newspaper clipping, staring and then sobbing. Shit ma, that was years ago. Who cares any more. But she does. She wants me back. Back in my locked bedroom with the piles of clothes and books and papers that she could never stand – or understand. That article too; it makes me puke. All that shit about honors student and most promising this and that. Nothing about gothgirl with the black lipstick and the raven fixation. Or the blonde bimbo with the mouth full of boy. Or scholar girl with the flaxen hair and the satchel squished tight with books. Nothing about the real me. Or the real me's – all of them prickly with pride

2. Back at the Dorm

Back at the dorm, I take a dip. The pool's just right, always. I wash the earth off me. The earth, with all its anger and anxieties, pissed off people playing with guns, all that crap that passes for life. It always feels wonderful, better than wonderful. What is it about the water here? It's like warm olive oil smoothly flowing over your skin, and without any kind of greasy shit you'd get at home if you spilled it. Remind me to ask Brad about that will you? Brad or maybe Sonya.

Sonya showed up at the crash site. Not that I paid the slightest attention. She told me later. I was wandering about the riverside, admiring stuff. It looked so lovely and I guess I thought I was still buzzed. Well, it was more fun than staring at Eric moaning and bleeding – side of his head all smashed. Yuck! I had to walk away. Out in the middle of nearly nowhere, not a house in sight and my cell at home, hiding under something or other.

That was the first thing that shoulda made me think. Hint #1: I'm walkin' away, saying to myself, *Where the fuck is that cell?* and suddenly I'm at home gazing at the pile of extremely valuable crap I wouldn't let my mother touch – sweaters, jeans, cloaks and socks and shit. God, it was in there somewhere. Then I worried about poor Eric and I'm back there at the wreck.

Another car comes by, squeals to a stop and backs up; just enough action to occupy my frazzled brain. A guy jumps out; he's about fifty, kinda chubby, looked like my math teacher, Mr. Frisell, balding at the front, and runs over, right past me, like I wasn't there. Hint # 2: He looks real close at Eric and then at someone next to him slumped over. He shakes his head and takes out his own cell.

I watch him make a call. Like the dumb chick that only takes notes, I stand there as he takes a hanky to Eric's head, dabbing away carefully. I feel my own head – seems okay. Nonplussed to say the very least, I stumbled off again. A kind of light-footed stumble at that – floaty almost, as if I wasn't quite connecting with the ground. Bit like E. The rapids we'd come to look at seemed as lovely as ever, and I crouched there trying to be so absorbed I wouldn't have to figure out the exact whereabouts of what I used to call my intelligence. It didn't work.

Eric's in that car bleeding and I'm out here watching the rapids: what does that tell you, girl? That I'm the luckiest chick alive? That I'm a selfish bitch who doesn't give a damn for her best high school buddy? That got me going back to the car. The Mr. Frisell lookalike was still cradling Eric and holding what looked like an old towel to his temple, only this time he was seated on a fold-out canvas thing, like as not retrieved form the trunk of his car. Eric sure didn't have one. I stood real close and apologized. Then I thanked him for all his kindness. He didn't seem to notice me. At first, that seemed to mean I wasn't worth paying attention to; since that was my dad's attitude half the time, I wasn't surprised. Then I wondered if he was deaf. There was deaf girl at school who could only talk if she was close enough to read your lips. I moved around to stand in front of him; he stared right through me. Then I got mad, told him to *Fuck off then*, and stomped off.

The ambulance peeled by seconds later, screeched to a stop and backed up, exactly like the Frisell lookalike. A guy and a chick flew out and began to do their thing. As they were loading Eric into the back, a cop car pulled up. I'm not crazy about cops, even if they're cute, which some of them are, so I hopped in to sit with Eric. The ambulance crew disappeared and we were alone. I said, *Eric, you're pretty fucked up dude, but you're gonna pull through, I know it.* I held his hand real tight as I was saying it. We were friends not lovers so this was a stretch. And he like totally disapproved of my love life, so touching was like *verboten*. He was not gonna be one of those guys I got it on with.

3. Sweat

So I'm jabbering on about how he's gonna make it and I'll be with him all the way when I notice his hand keeps slipping through mine. Thinking I'm sweaty with fear, I rub my hand on my sleeve. Sweat's one of my no-nos. As my gran would say, *Can't abide that.* There's a lot of stuff my gran can't abide: preachers, Republicans, store-bought jam – tons more too. She's one of those dyed-in-the-wool, Massachusetts liberals. Not one of those Mayflower wannabes, snooping about your garden party, making sure all the guests are up to snuff, but a liberal through and through. Goes on and on about the three E's: Equality, Education and Employment. Thinks Roosevelt was the last president with *any* kind of vision and moral fiber. Says Nixon was *all mob right from the start,* Kennedy – a *horny Catholic,* Clinton – *just plain horny,* Reagan – *a reprobate,* and the Busboys, well, *oil, they're slimy with it.* Last time she said that to me, after Thanksgiving dinner, while Dad walked the dogs and Mom washed the dishes and my brothers shot some nets out back, I looked at her and said, *Dee, you say slimy with it as if it was semen or something.* She stared at me with that old testament fervor, though Dad says it's just early Dylan, and he should know, he took her to that Town Hall concert in '64 that's just came out on CD, and said *it's worse, at least semen caries the seed of life, they wager profit out of slaughter.*

Me, I'm easy to please; it's just sweat and society in general that sucks. And this time the sweat would just not go away. I rubbed and rubbed, but Eric's hand slipped out of mine over and over. What a piss-off. Then the attendants were back with a stretcher with a bundle under a blanket – another body. *Did we hit someone?* I asked Eric. No use; he was out of it. *Oh my god,* I thought. *We've killed some poor person crossing the road in the dark.* Here's Eric, half-dead, and this stranger really dead. Shit, we're gonna wind up in jail. Careless driving while cooked; we'd only shared one dried shroom and were really just pleasantly buzzed, but they'd do blood tests and make examples of us. There'd been a surprise locker check just last month and three guys had stashes. Friend of mine just sold the last of hers, like, *an hour before*. She cried all through lunch.

Curiosity? Compassion? Or a bit of both? I guess the last, but as the ambulance started up and away, I leant over to pull back the blanket for a peek. Sweat again – couldn't lift it. Tried again; this time my hand went right though the blanket to the body – it was cold. Eek! Didn't try that again; sat with sleeping Eric all the way to the hospital; followed them into emergency and watched the drama unfold – Just like ER. Place was jammed with what some writers would call the dregs of humanity. While they readied Eric for what would likely be surgery, I wandered about, looking at them all, studying them. Ya! The stories behind every face! I felt like I could read the lives. Weird! That's why I wanted to be a writer; there's so many stories to tell, and not one like another! What I wouldn't give for a notebook and a pen. Holy synchronicity, there was one right there on a table with magazines! Cool pen too! Thank you, Carl Jung. I picked up, flipped it open, wrote the date and started.

I was so excited; I never noticed how easily I held pen and notebook. No sweat there. Hint #3: Emerg was packed, people moaning and bleeding and staring into space, children sleeping in their mothers arms, some of them whimpering – no one screaming, thank God. I was there for ages – totally forgot about Eric. Had pages and pages of notes when I noticed that dawn was coming up. *Shit, where's Eric?* thinks I, and wham, I'm in a room with a body in a bed. It's him all right, all bruised and bandaged and sleeping like a baby. Can't think what else to do, so I start taking notes on him. Then the chair starts to feel real comfortable, so I put my feet on the edge of the bed and shut my eyes, thinking I'll wake up when he does.

But I dream of my bedroom. I'm looking for something, but I

can't remember what. Then I move downstairs – place is empty and tidy as a museum. I'm floating kinda. Now that I can't find or even recall what I'm looking for, nothing seems to matter. I go through a window and into the garden. Wait a minute, I go *through* a window? How can that be? Curtains and all? I squat under my favorite tree and ponder. I was asleep in a chair by Eric's bedside, right, and then I must've started dreaming. But this dream is so real. Realer than real. And then I floated through the window. Must be a dream, then.

Then I'm back beside Eric, but he's still out of it. A nurse is checking in on him, fiddling with this and that and writing stuff down on a clipboard. She doesn't see me somehow, even though I move my legs and apologize. Eric's mother and father come in. They're really upset looking. I get up to say hello and they just totally ignore me. Mrs. Phillips sits down in the chair I was in, like I'd never been there. She never liked me much but never quite took it that far before. They stare at their bandaged sleeping son and weep. Well, she sobs and he comes over and stands with his hands on her shoulders. Their grief is so private, I have to leave. I walk to the door to exit, but my hand can't seem to grip the handle. And it's not just sweat this time, it goes right though – cuts through like a knife in warm butter. I stand there, too dumb to move. Suddenly, the door opens from the other side. It, I dunno, sweeps right through me, and a doctor comes in. I watch him walk over to Eric's parents and lean over to quietly talk. It seems like none of my business so I leave, trying not to freak over the door thing.

I say 'freak', but I still had the presence of mind to hang onto my notes and pen. Maybe they were my anchor – my anchor to sanity. A pretty wonky sanity I guess, but it was the best I could do at the time. I wander about the corridors for a bit. Hospitals are interesting places. I used to hate them, such a downer to spend any time there at all, but now I was fascinated by everything I saw. Even nurses at stations filling out forms and answering phones seemed interesting. Just like the Emerg, it was as if I could read their lives, like the details were just falling out of their brains as I went past: the argument they had with their husband, the problems their kids were having at school, what they were planning for supper, lingerie they wanted to buy. I walked about like an angel in a daze. I'd seen some TV show where someone in surgery had had an out of body experience while under anesthetic and like some lost spirit, wandered about the place till it wore off and he woke up. At one point, in his wanderings, he met up with a young girl wanderer, who was even more messed up than he was and cried in his arms. He figured she was out of her body like he was and said you're in for an operation aren't you, let's go find your body and you can go back in. I thought it was so cool and heroic of him. When they'd found the operating rooms and went through them, one at a time, looking for her, and couldn't, he'd twigged – she must have died in surgery and not known. He'd sat her down to discuss it, trying to discover how long ago her operation actually was. She didn't know or couldn't remember and just clung to him in fear. He was in for a triple bypass himself and his was one of the bodies they'd looked at while trying to find hers. He said something to her about guardian angels and maybe she had one who could take her to heaven. What did she think about that? he asked, trying to cheer her up. She looked up from her whimpering and seemed to be thinking it over. Then this really cool-looking lady shows up out of nowhere – gentle and kind and soft – in a beautifully cut, pale cream dress, and asks Marcie if she'd like to come with her. And Marcie's just so blown away that this stranger knows her name that she gets up off the guy's lap and takes the lady's hand. The lady thanks the guy for his help and they turn about and walk away. The guy kinda smiles to himself, no doubt thinking a job well done, and then gets up, walks back to the operating theatre, goes between the docs and the nurses and sorta slides back into his body.

In the next scene, he's waking up with his wife and sons at the bedside. They're happy he's made it. In all the happy family stuff, he pulls his wife down to his face and whispers *I met a dead girl and gave her to an angel*. She smiles and says she's proud of him in a way that makes you think she doesn't believe it but wants to humor him.

4. Ally Walks In

I was sitting on a couch in a little room at the end of a corridor, by a window looking out onto the parking lot, thinking over all this when Ally walked in, doing her usual *Hey Mel what's happening?* routine. She sits down beside me and starts on about her hair and how she doesn't like it like this; what do I think? And I just scream; after all I've been through, this I just can't take. *Ally,* I squeal, *you're dead. You got cancer last year!*

Mel, she squeals back. *Guess what? You're dead too! You blew it in Eric's car!*

Course, I thought, she was shittin' me. I was no more dead than… what? I sure didn't feel dead. Ally went on to explain that no one ever feels dead, that's the big trick it plays on you. You're dead and just don't know it. Especially if it happens quickly, like with me. Some don't know it for years. She knew because of all the exhaustion from the cancer. Suddenly, one morning she felt, like, a hundred times stronger. She knew she couldn't be sick any more, she felt so good, so she just had to be dead. It didn't make any sense, she knew, but that's how she knew.

So we exchanged a bunch more notes, I told her how sad everyone was after she died and what her old beaus were up to, but she knew it all anyway. It was just like she'd never been away, like when Sonja went to stay with her aunt in Italy for a year but emailed every day and didn't miss a thing.

So you guessed it, Ally takes me to heaven and I settle down and live happily ever after? Well, not really. It was really cool, the place she took me too, a bit kinda suburban-shopping-mally, like way too much redesigning-the-den and not nearly enough party-till-you-puke. It was heaven enough for her, but Ally always was getting her hair done and shopping with her mother. After staying at a youth hostel place for a bit, I confronted her on it. Her guardian angel lady had just finished with one of her inspiring pep talks, which Ally just seemed to lap up (substitute mother figure I thought) and I blurted *Ally I gotta get outta here, it's driving me crazy!*

She was like *Well, okay. What do you want me to do?*

I dunno, I yelled. *I got a life to live and this place makes me feel dead already!*

And she yells, *You are dead already you stupid bitch, get used to it!*

I gave her the finger and ran out the door and down the hall, running past at least two guys I'd slept with in the past week just to try and feel normal again, catching up with the guide lady on the path outside.

She turned to me like she was expecting me and said something about me needing a little more challenge and excitement in my heaven life. Stunned, I said *Sure, take me to it!* And that's how I ended up in this experimental college in the foothills here, in this seriously cool dorm that snakes over the ground like a sleeping reptile and the windows are huge and full of forest.

I was gonna say that sort of brings you up to speed, but no, not really. And why do I want to bring you up to speed anyway? Because you'll have a hard enough time believing I'm dead at all. I don't blame you; I had a hard time believing it myself – still do. It's this whole myth that society makes you swallow, about death and all that. Two myths actually, both equally wrong – the church myth and the science myth. The church one says only the goody-goodies get to go and when they get there it's all *praise the lord* and *piss on the devil*. The science one says there is nothing afterwards, that it's all religious bullshit – crap dreamed up by churches to keep you in line, paying taxes and slaves to the church. And if you feel anything else, it's drugs or your brain needing a bit more or a bit less oxygen.

To be honest, I could see the drugs argument a bit. Mushrooms make you feel like God and everything else, wildly alive and vibrating like crazy. Every kid in the world knows that, and all those Woodstock types do too, if you can get them to admit it.

Eric's Uncle Dennis, who only came to visit once, riding his Harley all the way from Arizona, told us. He took us for pizza and said, like he was asking about the weather, *You kids doing psychedelics yet?* I had the feeling, if we'd said no, he'd have said *Why not*? But we fessed up, least I did and Eric meekly followed. His next line, *Did you ever ball high?* really embarrassed Eric, as he's not, like, a sexual guy, but it got me interested, though I tried to act dumb. I wondered if maybe he was making a pass, but he didn't seem like the type – you know, the horny type. He seemed like he had his hormones balanced back in Arizona. Eric said he had a woman that he lived with – a yoga teacher or something – but that they'd never met her. I don't know why but I trusted him. When he was telling us this stuff it was never like he was weird or something. He looked you in the eye, but gently, like he cared. There was a couple of times while we were there, munching away, that I swore he was reading my mind. He seemed to anticipate just what I was gonna say somehow, but, like, never used it to get one up on me, you know?

We explained we were buddies not lovers. Dennis said we oughta be as our vibrations matched up good or something. I laughed and told him not to go all Shirley MacLaine on us. He laughed too, and said he wasn't, just that we made a good match. But hell, it was none of his business anyway – he shouldn't have butted in. He said old hippies were like that. I'll never forget what he said then: *We're just dying to get the kids on our side before they get irretrievably jived by the mainstream culture.*

Eric told him not to worry, we were cool, we'd seen *Easy Rider* and we had all the Kevin Smith movies on DVD.

I said, *Sure, and Michael Moore too.*

Then we got into movies. He said they lived way out there and couldn't get into town much, but collected video off satellite. I told him he kept reminding me of that wingy hippie couple in that David Russell film, the one before *Three Kings*, where the guy goes on the pilgrimage to find his birth mother and they wind up in New Mexico or Arizona in some totally crazy situation, but he hadn't seen it. For ages afterwards I imagined his woman to be the Lily Tomlin crazy in the film.

And movies get you into all that conspiracy theory stuff, which Eric is like totally into – got all the sites bookmarked; you know that kid that got all the secret shit out by using the FOI act? The Vault guy? Emails him regularly; stands up and reads bits from *From the Wilderness* in history class; drives his father crazy at supper arguing about shit; his dad reads the *New York Times* and just won't accept that half the writers are CIA assets, or were once. He drives him even crazier by saying shit like, *Well at least they're not operatives*. Eric really opened up with this; *It's his bag,* as Dennis said. All that hippie talk, it's so cute. I wished he was wearing his *Police State* t-shirt, I'd have been so proud, but Dennis rolled into town on short notice (no notice actually); just sort of appeared at the door and freaked his dad out; they hadn't spoken in years – some kinda falling out over the Reagan years, support for the Contras or the opposite, I can't remember. Even Eric had to research it – before our time, don't you know. Oh yeah, I remember now; Eric tracked it down; the Agency was smuggling crack into East LA and using the profits to arm the death squads. And wouldn't you know, the guy that exposed it lost his job, or got demoted to counting the staples on Sundays and holidays. Way the cookie crumbles dude – *Unless you're connected by the tongue to the asshole,* like Dennis said. Man, that guy was so cool. *Is* so cool, but I'll get to that later.

Which brings me back to the Woodstock types; Dennis was the best example of the kind you can get to talk. Eric's dad, Brian, and mine, Larry, they're the closet types; got scared straight way back when and won't admit it, neither of them. Brian's a corporate lawyer and Larry's real estate – driven talents, the two of them. And both, weirdly enough, came back from their wanderings and married high school sweethearts, one a kindergarten teacher and the other a nurse. Larry spent three years living alone in a cabin in the woods in Oregon, hunting, growing veggies, chopping wood; can't get him to talk about it now; why he did it, or why he stopped – won't budge, no matter what I say. Mom says he just wanted to be like Thoreau.

Wrong coast, I tell her.

Wanted to get away from his parents, she whispers. He once made a joke about ending up like the Unabomber. But that was as he was walking out the door with the dogs after a couple of belts of Wild Turkey on New Year's, and probably doesn't count. Shit, I can talk; I was cooked myself, on my way to party.

And who knows about Brian? Eric sure doesn't, and it's not for lack of trying. Eric wonders if he got turned off with the Kennedy coup. I say *no, he's way too young*; couldn't have been more than ten when it happened. More like a Vietnam thing. Didn't he demonstrate? We think he was in Canada all the time. Mom says *you get him loaded and he can talk French like a native.* I say *Right, your dad loaded, like when?* Mom says he helped smuggle Canadian pot into Maine for the anti-war movement. And got caught? No; made so much money they argued about splitting it up and someone got hurt. A draft dodger, drug smuggler? No, he got a teaching job in some small college in the boonies – all legit. My dad went to college too – thesis on the Transcendentalists; I'm proud of that. Then Thoreau in the woods, then corporate law. How weird is that? Oh yeah, fit my mom in there somewhere – the nurse with the wound. Wound she can't see I say.

Holy shit! Am I ever rambling. Talking about the old days does that. But maybe it helps you see the state I'm in now.

5. The State I'm In Now

I guess that's sorta happy, way happier than I bet a lot of you would've suspected, but still connected to family and friends. I know that sounds like, happy-go-lucky – the feelin' groovy riff, over and over till you feel like puking – and so suspect because I was not so easygoing on earth. Yeah, Little Miss Neurosis with her creative outlets, more like. But a lot of that shit seems so gone now. Not all of it, but, like, a lot of it. What am I now? Still young, still confused, still searching, but like, way more at ease, way more cool, and I mean really cool, not fake cool.

I know what I am; I'm an American in Heaven, and I'm here to give you the straight goods. No church crap, no science lies, and you know what, no bipartisan subcommittees either; just Americans hanging out in Heaven, or at least some Americans in one of the Heavens.

Sonya, that's the one who showed up at the crash site but got ignored by Little Miss Stoner Chick, tells me there's lots of Heavens, not just the one I'm in. There's kind of a different Heaven for everyone, depending on what you expect and what you're comfortable with. Lots of hells and places in between too, if you're interested. Sonya's seen most of them, and what she hasn't seen Brad's seen. Brad's her partner – at least that's the way they act. They're guides, right? What I don't get is that they've got a guide too. Guides with guides – too weird – but I haven't met her yet, just heard how seriously cool she is.

Sonya says a lot of stuff that seems pretty wild to me. I just kinda nod and listen, thinking I'll figure it out one day. Like there's a lot of forgiveness and backwards and forwards in time stuff I just don't get. Don't even wanna think about it. You know how many, like, criminals are wandering about here? Unbelievable. On their best behavior too. If the punishment fits the crime, as somebody said somewhere, then that little truth sure don't apply here. Sonya says punishment is for the earth. I asked how does it work then, with all these crazies walking about; not that they're crazy now, but when you hear about what they did... She said it's when we go back that we make reparations.

That's like sowing and reaping right?

Yeah, she says, *and you can call it karma in action too.*

Karma, says I, *that's one of those new-age words, right?*

No, it's one of those ancient, almost forgotten words, she says grinning. She reminds me of this friend of my mother's, this nurse chick that never married and works with the aids people – kinda know-it-all smug, if you know what I mean. Like, for an example, I was sipping a juice in a café a while back with one of those eager boys, eager dead boys that is, and a guy he must've known kinda slips in beside us. We were talking about clubs and parties and stuff, trying to avoid the usual depressing parent stuff, something we all have to handle one way or another and this guy mentions the guy he stabbed in a fight and how they're like best friends now. The guy I'd been sitting with, he did seem like, you know, from the wrong side of town, and I should've guessed he'd know people like that. I was never into that violence thing and none of my friends were either. We just avoided people like that. We only went to certain malls and theatres, and house parties were strictly by invitation only – you know, secret society stuff. Even the jocks, who I used to party with a bit, learned to tame themselves, once the ground rules were like, firmly in place.

So the story was that he had been cornered in an alley on the way home from school by a bunch of guys and the dealer dude over a drug debt – like something really stupid, twenty bucks maybe – but he's the only one with a knife, and sure he uses it and the dealer bleeds to death and he takes off when he's got the chance. The knife goes up some tree in a buddy's back yard and he has a shower before his mom comes home from work. He skips school next day and heads downtown, trying to figure why the cops haven't showed. He somehow steals a twenty from a homeless guy, takes off, and later gets into a club and, believe it or not, finds another stash in the washroom, buys some bad E, dances till he drops, dies in the ambulance, where his nemesis (I said that – he's too dumb) is waiting. And like ghosts who don't know they're ghosts, they fight till they get bored and then head out together to discover the world.

Months of big fun ensue. You thought I didn't know words like ensue, didn't ya? I've heard a lot of these stories since comin' here, but I'll have to admit, theirs was one of the best, probably because they had each other. Lot of us wandered about alone, not knowing there was anyone else dead to hang with, just all these live bodies ignoring us. They did the prankster thing for ages, screwing people up all over once they'd realized they could speed about the country like bullets (that's what he said, I'd never use that kind of word). After, like, months of fooling around, tripping people up and moving stuff around and what all, they kinda get to thinking that maybe if they looked hard enough they'd find Heaven somewhere.

By this time, of course, they know they can fly all over: oceans and mountains and shit, right; so they're like, everywhere, looking and looking, all serious and searching, and finding people everywhere doing regular stuff, working, playing sports, walking, sleeping, but not really accomplishing much other than looking. Then they think, *Hey maybe churches are where it's at.* Sonya says a lot of kids go through that phase. So they do that thing, every one they can find, and I guess that includes temples and synagogues, but they're not the kind of guys to know those words.

They sit through every kind of service imaginable, I guess. Somewhere, at some service, some guide, in disguise I guess, wanders up to them and says – dig this – *You guys about through with fuckin' around?* First off, they're so amazed anyone has recognized them that they just sit silent. Then they both say *Sure* at the same time. The way they describe this guy makes me think of Mickey Rourke in a black leather jacket. Course, they didn't say that, not being movie buff types by nature, but he sure sounded about that level of cool. So then it's the old story; he's got their attention and from there it's just a quick hop to Heaven.

So the point of all that was, what? Oh yeah, to show you how people that'd be behind bars on earth get to wander about free here. There's no, like, punishment stuff happening, least not that I can see. It's like if you can behave yourself in public you get to roam about and do just what you want. That guy is just one example. Trust me, there's lots of them. And that includes some of those school shooters. I even saw one of them, never mind who, sitting with one of the victims like they were the best of friends. Sonya had pointed them out to me the day before – not that we have *days* or *before* here really, we have, you know, ongoing life. Like, things happen, things happen all the time, but it's not like days or weeks or years. Sure, you get up and you walk around and talk and stuff, but it's not like time passes. It's like *here we are now* and then another *here we are now*, and then another until it's all just *here and now.* Does that make any sense? Probably not but it's the best I can do.

So the day after (ha-ha) Sonya points these two out, I go over to speak with them. Instead of bullshitting about the bush, I tell them straight off that I heard they were involved in one of the school shootings. One of them goes *Yeah, so*? (the girl, doing the chick thing, even here.)

Well, I said, *I was wondering why you're sitting here together, aren't you like enemies?*

Then he says, *We used to be, but not now.*

Then she says, *We've talked things over and we both see where we could've done better. We just weren't reaching out.*

Cliques, right?

They both nod, *yeah.*

Insults, taunting, you know the story. *But why the guns?* I ask the guy, confident.

He shrugs. *It was really the only way out for us. We were so down we figured there was no place else to go, so why not take them with us in a blaze of glory. It's the American way.*

I thought, *Heard that one before and I still don't buy it,* but just nodded. But the trouble with here is that often you can't have the thoughts you want 'cause people pick upon them. Maybe not exactly, not every word, but they get the general idea, and you're left looking like a fool. Don't know if they picked up much, not everyone seems to be clued in, but you can never tell. The chick wasn't really one of the victims, I know because I asked her and lived through her reply – like, the attitude of her reply. She was at a dentist appointment on the big day, but took an overdose to be with her friend who had been shot. Her suicide had been kept out of the papers. She looked at the guy, kinda wiry and geeky to be honest, and said she thought she hated him in school, but now knows she secretly loved him. I kept my *stupid slut* thoughts to myself until I walked away – give that relationship about ten minutes. She made me think of those women that write to guys on death row, fall in love and marry them while they run through all their appeals.

Still, you see what I mean? Unless people are at each other's throats, which I've never seen, there's no, like, law of the land to keep them apart. When I queried Sonja on this she promised to take me to another level where that kind of action was par for the course. Levels – we got a lot of those here. Sonja says they're like floors on an elevator: once you know the elevator's operational you can use it anytime to go anywhere. Lots of folk don't know about it though, especially the ones on the lower floors. They think the one they're on is the only one. I was like that myself until she took me for a ride.

It's not really an elevator, right, but the effect is kind of the same. Once you've decided it's like immediate; think and you're there. But you have to know what to think of, and if you don't, then nothing. Sonja knew what to think of. We were like suddenly walking towards a small town from the country. I could see it just ahead – buildings and shit. But as I looked around the area we were in looked more like a park – you know, planned, but not too planned, like a park that someone wants to look like the country. Sonja picked up my confusion and told me that it was a big park in the middle of one of the lower astral cities. For some reason I thought that meant piles of used condoms and syringes and smelly old people sleeping on benches.

There are some homeless people here, Sonja added to my thought, *mostly ones who don't really know they're dead. Some do, but they all seem to want something they recognize, so we've put up shelters that are only slightly more luxurious than they'd have on earth.* The buildings turned out to be – guess what? – houses and stores and stuff I wasn't sure about. Some looked okay, kinda, and others looked crappy, almost boarded up – an anywhere kind of downtown. Some people walked around, all of them minding their own business; no eye contact; scowls instead of smiles. The sidewalk was the sidewalk, the road was the road. Cars parked, a few going by like they had nowhere special to go.

Grumpytown I called it.

Sonja laughed, *Yeah, I guess.*

We walked into a store – variety store, sort of – Korean guy at the counter, tryin' to smile. We bought some gum and some candy. Well, Sonja did. I was the silent partner in this, like, *oh-so-normal* transaction. Sonja paid (like she actually had cash in her pocket). On our level no one used money so I couldn't figure out where she got it. Later she told me she just imagined it and it was there.

Like counterfeit?

No, like real.

Sounds like magic to me.

It was in a way, she said. By then we were outside again. But she said, *Hey, I've got an idea. Wait just a minute.* She disappeared inside and I looked about till she came back with the news that the game was just a block away. The game was non-stop poker, played for big stakes.

We walked a block and turned down an alley. The first door she tried was locked. The second opened up and we poked our way in – dim and smelly. Ugh! I wanted outta there. But Sonja said to hang loose, that it could be useful for me. A big guy appeared in front of us, blocking the way. I thought *Oh shit, it's gonna get ugly.* But Sonja smiled and leant over to whisper something in his ear. Whatever it was it made him relax and let us pass. I didn't fancy blowin' anyone in there just to get a look at some dead guys playin' poker, probably none of them had washed in a week, but I kept my mouth shut. Sonja, of course, heard my thought and said, *Don't sweat it, we're cool.*

Down a small set of stairs and we were in poker central – about four tables playin' and guys standin' around watching – seemed like everyone was smoking cigarettes and cigars. Holy crow that place stank! No one so much as glanced at us, but I was tense, I don't mind telling you. I'm not stupid; places like this either got busted or got taken down by rival gangs. What was I supposed to be learning? The words *just watch* appeared in my brain. Well, I watched and watched. Those guys sure were into it. Each table had piles of money on it. Every once in a while one of the guys would rake it over his way and a new round would begin – a few nods, grunts and grimaces. Sonja led me out; we passed the big bruiser on the way; guys like that usually give me a second look at least. This one didn't.

As we wandered about after this, I was stuck between wanting to see it all and see it all *now* and going right back to our level and staying there. This level sure sucked but, you know, I was curious. Around a corner and we came across an old lady curled up on the sidewalk. Not seeing her till the last minute, I kicked her by mistake. She growled and raised her head, looked up at us and growled again then held out a gloved hand. Sonja gave her some coin and knelt down to say something. I thought I heard her say *not for me,* but I couldn't be sure. Sonja then pulled out a small bottle of liquor and gave it to her – deep pockets that Sonja. The old girl grasped it tightly and lay back down to sleep. We stepped over her. I didn't wanna be the whiny bitch so I kept my mouth shut about the stink. Sonja said she likely doesn't know she's dead. *Froze somewhere, stayed unconscious and was floated here by guides.*

How long would she have to stay around here, I asked.

As long as she needs to was the answer. I didn't quite get that but didn't want to, like, admit it. This sure was a dumpy section of town; almost everything was boarded up, or looked empty.

Run down is how they like it, Sonja answered my thought, *It's what they're comfortable with.* That makes sense to me now, but back then it didn't, so if it seems screwy to you I suggest you lay back and wait for more.

Next thing I know we're slap bang into an argument – four or five guys yelling and waving their fists about. Didn't get the language at all, but the vibe was plain – fuck you asshole. Raggy clothes, smelly breath and that no-shave-since-Christmas look. We stepped around them carefully, but we might as well have been invisible.

We can do that too if you want, said Sonja to my thought. At least it felt like she did. She had this way of putting her words right inside my head (more about that later); first the invisible thing: I asked her to explain. Well, she could throw a shield of invisibility around us no problem, and no, she wasn't a sorceress, it was just one of things you could learn in the afterlife, and although you might not want to do it where we lived, down here it could be useful sometimes. Sounded like a blast, I could hardly wait. This was still the early days, when my basic adjustment had been to get a social life and leave it at that. Except for those depressing visits back to earth, my death had been more like a vacation than anything else. I'd been having so much fun, it never occurred to me that there'd be a lot to learn. Sonja'd check in once in a while, joke around a bit and then split.

Did I want to see a soup kitchen type place? Sure, why not? Pretty soon we were standing in one, looking at sad types shuffling around and sipping at soup and noodles. Sonja seemed to know everyone in the place – the workers too – and moved about, chatting. Me, tailing her, not quite sure who to look at – bit teenagerish really. I can still do that sometimes. It's like I slip into this hole and can't get out no matter what.

Really it was just like what you'd expect one of those places to be, if you'd ever given it any thought, which I hadn't. I mean, who wants to think about the homeless? It's not what people in the burbs do; we keep our houses clean and our lawns mowed. That's like our job in life. Not that anyone gives a shit; we're the ones that get shit on, just for minding our own business. Everyone does it: the rich, the poor, the politicians, the artists. If you don't have a loft downtown or a country estate you're nobody. Gees, I sound like my mom. Girl's worst fear that: turning-into-mommy-itis.

After the shelter, we walked around a bit, and seemed to come to a classier section of town. Sonja said she was going to throw the invisibility shield round us. I said *Cool, let's go for it*. Not that I noticed anything much different. Everything looked the same, so did Sonja. But when we walked into this place, looked like an old hotel, nobody seemed to notice us. There was a bar in the lobby, with a few guys on stools sippin' beers. Ladies too actually, didn't notice them at first. Big palm trees, coupla couches, usual lobby type thing. Sonja said, *Go right up to them and stick your tongue out.*

Didn't need any more encouragement than that; went up to a small wiry guy in a suit who seemed pretty tight with the honey blonde next to him, stuck my face between them and blew into his right nostril; no reaction: nothing. Did the same to her; laughed – howled actually. Sonja motioned to me and we went over to the check-in counter. I couldn't resist climbing on it and doin' a little dance. Sonja jumped up and joined me. My feet came so close to the clerk's face, I couldn't believe it. We laughed and laughed. I dug Sonja for that. She coulda been a teach bitch but no, she was my buddy.

I knew there had to be a reason for the invisibility thing, but didn't find out till we got upstairs. Every room, or at least every room we went into, had a chick in it about my age, usually lounging around in a slip, smoking and looking bored. A couple were busy porking or blowing some guy. After a while, I looked at Sonja and said, *So what, I know about this shit. Chicks get into hooking, happens all the time.*

Sonja said that wasn't the whole story. They were stuck there she said. She removed the shield; wanted to go into this room and talk to this girl she knew – girl named Sonja wouldn't you know. She was in a halter top and tight shorts and those stacked sandals, smoking what smelt like pot and grinnin' that stoner grin.

Hey Sonja what's happenin'? kinda set the tone. My Sonja tried not to be the earnest do-gooder lady but she didn't do too good a job, far as I could see. Sonja had her great pot, a seriously cool wardrobe and a boyfriend who picked her up every day at five, and you know what, doing strangers didn't bother her that much. Hey, it was a life and better than some she'd seen. My Sonja tried all this I-can-show-you-a-better-existence-and-you're-free-to-do-what-you-want stuff but it just didn't wash. Sonja had been on the street, that's after the usual shitty childhood crap, before getting abducted, raped and cut up for a dumpster on earth, so the hooker shit she was doin' now was real high class in comparison. And it was obvious they'd had this same conversation about ten times already. She even asked me if I wanted to stick around and have some fun. And, to tell you the truth, I felt like a nun sayin' no.

Sonja wanted me to see a couple more chicks, but it was the same story over and over. Well, just about; one girl looked kinda bruised but said she liked a little s&m once in a while. So what if it got a little out of hand; no one was forcing her, and besides, she got in a couple of good shots herself. Back on the street, invisible again, Sonja and I debated this whole victim thing. Surely, a victim was only a victim if she felt like one. If someone else tells her she's a victim when she feels like a winner, what's the point? Sonja said she understood what I was getting at, but really just wanted me to see how things were on this level, as opposed to the one we were on. And even though I was caught up in the discussion, I had to thank her for that.

Anyway, next thing I know we're headed back to that park and once there she grabs my hand and we're like, whoosh, back to where I hang out, wherever that is.

6. Bummers

It's horrible to say, but after you've been here awhile, and settling into the endless vacation style fun, it's like totally the worst experience to go back to earth and face the music. Everyone you see is so damn depressed! Family and most of your friends, not the fakes who just wanted the status, they're like the saddest bunch of sacks you ever seen. Man, the shit I'll pull to avoid going there! The shit everyone pulls. You know those dweeby dimwit cousins you just hated to visit, but your mom said you had to, because it was your dad's brother and they'd been so tight since they were kids'n all, and after all, Baltimore really did have its charms? Well, worse than that – way worse. This is like bummed out junkies in a funeral parlor waitin' for the man. And then there's Eric.

God, poor Eric. After two surgeries, it still looks like he's gonna be paralyzed from the waist down – the rest of his life in a wheelchair. Talk about fates worse than death. Used to say that when I was still, as you guys say, *alive*; picked it up as an attitude from adults I guess, but now that I'm here I can, like, really assure you that it's so true. Eric's in prison, man, and I'm in Heaven. It sucks! Totally! Course what sucks even more is I have to visit him and, like, spill all this crap about how it's a challenge he can face up to, and how spirit will really help him if he takes it on and all. All stuff I've been told to say, you know, by those in the know. What I want to say is, *Eric! fuck it! Jump out of that window, make sure it's head first, and I'll take you to where it's all happening*. Then Sonja says, like in my head, because she's not there, but we had the argument already, *what about his parents and brother, they'd be even more messed up than they are now*, and I sink back into my screw-it-all-anyway thing.

Well, with that great news, let me move on to my family, that other endless source of fun. My brothers are like totally into whatever they're totally into – sports, chicks, dope, internet porn – and look kinda glad that I'm finally out of their way. We never did get on exactly. They were always like the opposing team: determined to win no matter what. Dad was like god to them, when they could get him, which wasn't much, with work and all. Then I come along – the little cutie that stole his heart – and they like hate me forever. Hate's not too strong a word. I know you're thinking *spoilt brat-bitch princess-loser,* but it wasn't like that, really. Dad really did love me more then them. I'm just more lovable that's all; a better person all round – cuter, smarter, more dignified. Born in the wrong family if you ask me. Sonja says I'm wrong on that count, but won't tell me why; says I'm not ready for it. I'll give her some slack on that one as she's so cool on any number of other issues, but really, no one likes being treated like a teenager, especially teenagers.

Mom's the worst in a way. I'll get this emotional tug sometimes, this weepy rope pulling at my waist and I'm reeled in like the catch of the day. And when I get to where she's at, it's like a grocery store or something equally loser-like. Last time it was the baby food section. She's standing there weeping, and I'm forced to stand beside her and watch. I say all the usual stuff we dead kids say: *It's okay mom, I'm here.* And, *Mom there's no need for this, I'm right here beside you.* And, *Mom please don't cry, please.* And, *Oh lady, get a life!* I put my arm around her shoulder, I hug her waist till I run my arms right through, I pull on her hair, none of it does any good; I'm like this hopeless, useless piece of schmooze. I follow her home, hoping she'll finally notice me, but she doesn't. Not a wasted trip entirely though; when we get there, Bewley, our golden lab, catches the vibe and licks her all over till she giggles a bit. Then she rolls around the carpet with him and feels better. I know he sees me 'cause he looks right at me with that lab grin they've got, and barks a bit. I wave back and he barks again. Mom just thinks he's excited, but doesn't shush him 'cause he's the best friend a housewife ever had, or so she says. After that phase she gets the wanna-look-in-the-photo-album vibe and I stand in front of her yelling *No! Mom, No! Let's not go there huh,* 'cause I know what that means, more weeping and wailing that I have to endure. Sometimes my ranting works and she changes her mind and starts working on supper. And sometimes she has a cigarette and watches a soap. Then I usually return to the land of love and light, as Sonja calls it, to resume my fun-filled deathlife.

Last time dad yanked on my chain, I found him at lunch with his secretary Andrea, mourning my loss. I knew it was hopeless, but I said it all the same, *Dad stop that, I'm right here real as can be.* What a great kid I'd been, a bit nutty, but all creative people are eccentric, he understood that, full of promise, such a great future ahead of me. Andrea added that it wasn't a waste really, that people went on and had lives in the afterlife. She watched that psychic guy, John Edward, and knew lots of stuff. Her own mother had had a near-death experience, met her grandmother in some garden, had a couple of laughs and came back all reassured and stuff. Dad said he wished he could believe that. I said *Believe it Dad I'm right fucking here in your face!* Then Andrea says *Maybe she's here with us now, who knows? She could be listening to us talk.* I turned to her shouting *Yes Andrea, right on, you got it!* She just looked at my dad, all intent and smiling, trying to, I dunno, lift his spirits I guess.

This Andrea, as well as being cute in a totally non-perky kind of way, was much smarter than I'd figured. Really though, I'd only met her once at an office barbeque thingee Dad had last summer, or maybe the summer before, shit, some summer *sometime,* and had been too busy being cool to notice her much. A couple of the others in Dad's office had dragged their families along and there were at least two guys with half a brain I was not totally disgusted with. I painted myself up and padded about – the gossamer goth princess. For some reason I couldn't figure, Andrea and Dad parted outside the restaurant, he to the office, she off home. Curious, I followed. From our perspective, earth pace is incredibly slow and dull, but if you're interested enough, you'll keep at it. Andrea took a bus, walked a bunch, stopped in a flower shop for some irises, chatted with the lady, who was obviously her friend, and walked home to her apartment. Nosy bitch that I am, I followed her right in. Sonja tells me to be careful with that kind of thing, that it can be addictive, not to mention just plain rude. I'll take my chances.

She fixed the flowers and settled down on the couch to admire them. She was so peaceful and quiet I wondered if something was wrong, but she just kept gazing at the flowers from her perch on the couch. Was this some kind of yoga meditation thing? Could be. Didn't know much about that, except for a couple of articles in a movie mag of my mom's; you know, celebs talking about their yoga teachers. But then a totally weird thing happened; something that looked just like Andrea floated up out of her body. There was one Andrea on the couch, cross-legged and still, and another in the same pose floating about three feet above. I'd hallucinated plenty before, but this didn't seem like that. This was like stereo, but with visuals. Then this second floaty Andrea unlocked her legs, stood straight, and floated over to me. Course I was floating too, but we ghosts do that all the time – it's part of being dead; one of the better parts if you ask me. Kinda startled and kinda pleased, I said *Hi Andrea, remember me?*

Sure do, she says, smiling. *Melanie, right? Met you at the barbeque. How are things with you now?*

I tell her pretty good really, but this sadness with my family really got to me.

But you're having a good life now, you're settled and all, right?

Yeah, I tell her, *I got a place and friends and stuff – it's cool.*

You look great, she says, all shiny and happy.

Course I had to sing a few lines of that REM song, *Shiny happy people holding hands,* but she didn't know it and it kinda fell flat. How could she see me, I wanted to know, when no-one else could?

It was easier to slip out of your body when meditating than most people realized, she told me. The hard part was remembering what your other self did while it was out. She said, *I'll go back in shortly but not recall much, if anything.*

You won't remember seeing me?

Probably not, it's so hard to carry the memories through. But I'll have a calm kind of assured feeling that you're okay and I'll try to convince your father of that when he gets here. I guess I must've looked surprised for she went on: *That's something you should know, he comes here sometimes. Oh-oh, it's time for me to go back in, sorry.* And she floated back in. Well no, kind of reinserted herself more like.

Her body on the couch started to, like, ripple a bit. Then she opened her eyes, which, to tell the truth, I hadn't noticed were closed anyway, and began to smile like there was something to be really happy about. For some reason I started wondering about Eric and right away I was in his room, watching him read. He was using a night-light, so maybe he'd fall asleep soon and I could talk to him. That's usually how we got together these days. We'd sit on the carpet in his bedroom and chatter away like the old days. It was usually fun so I was okay to wait around till he fell asleep. Other times I'd get there when he was already out and checking things out, but this time I'd get to see him separate from his sleeping body, like I did once with Mom.

I sat in his easy chair for the wait and must've slipped away myself as he was standing over me smiling when I opened my eyes. That's the best part really, him standing there, smiling down. He's, like, so buzzed about his working body. The one on the bed is broken, probably for good, but this spirit one is just fine. Sonja tells me all spirit bodies are in great shape, except for those in the lower realms that don't even know they're dead and carry their crippledness about with them. I want to argue with her on that one but figure she must know more than me and keep my mouth shut; funny one that, me keeping my mouth shut – never did that before. Guess death has affected me somehow. That death thing again – you'd have to be here like me to get it; you're just not dead, you're like so alive you could burst.

Eric agrees with me; we sit and talk about it for hours. Like, how could anyone call *this* dead? Both of us are better chess players, for example. Your brain just seems to work better. And we have the greatest talks too. It's just too bad when he goes back to his body. He goes, *Hey I'm waking up or something*, and floats over and reinserts himself. Sometime he just clicks out: gone, and I watch as he wakes up in that other body, the stranger, the enemy. Makes me so sad to watch him struggle that I have to go away. I'm just so lucky to be dead, can you understand that?

Maybe you can't and maybe I shouldn't think you oughta. I mean, I never could've when I was alive. Oh, I thought I could, sure; I had all these fantasies about sad, bloodless Goth girls floating around mausoleums and muttering imprecations to wilted flowers and writing poems to the angel of death, who I figured to be a sort of marvelously gnarled witchy type who enfolded herself in silvery wings after every utterance of sublime gloom. Turns out it's Sonja, in jeans and a *death sucks* t-shirt who finally grabs my attention and moves me to where I am now, which I'll have to admit is pretty cool really. It's just that, oh it's so damn frustrating, not being able to tell you what it's really like. Super alive? Alive to the max? More alive than you'll ever be? None of it sounds anywhere near right, and even Sonja's contribution, *bursting with vitality*, seems way too teacher-ish.

So you'll just have to take my word for it. Anyway, why would I lie to you? Okay, I guess that's dumb. I could easily be lying. Hey, maybe I'm the spawn of Satan sent to deceive all you dumb earthlings into thinking this paradise I'm living in is actually Heaven. Sonja says she's had more than her fair share of dead folk who think that. Usually she has to go get one the church-type guides for them. Apparently, folk that can quote the King James

Bible are really in demand here. Sonja isn't much for that, says she never was – way she was brought up – but it's great that there are plenty who were, as there's always Bible types coming through. *Thank God there's big chunks of Heaven set aside for everybody,* she says, *so they can keep out of each other's hair*. Sounds about right, but I have to tell you there's some Muslim girls around – still got their headdress, that's how I know. And some Buddha guys in their robes. And Chinese people doing Tai-chi in the park. That's because this is the spirit world nearest to North America, which is such a mixed society anyway, they all just kind of float up and land here in the same crazy mixture as before. But those that want to just be with their own kind can just move over to wherever and stay there. *There's lots of places like that,* Sonja says. *Replicas of the countries on earth with their native populations intact*. I should see them for myself I suppose, but there's so much to do here, you just can't get around to everything. But I will one day.

Most of the time I'm either havin'fun or chillin' out – blast really. Lotta kids are still into that teen town peer pressure bullshit, but it don't last long 'cause it doesn't get them where it used to. Girls can imagine the coolest outfit and suddenly it's there, on you, looking great. Hair too; I used to have the worst, dry, stringy, yucky, about four different shades of shit brown. Now I'm a silky smooth, Julianne Moore, honey blonde babe. I feel and look awesome, but so do the other four thousand plus other girls who had the same idea. I thought about going back to Goth black for about five seconds. That look just wouldn't work here. And that's another thing; you think just the chicks who died in the month before you are here? Think again, babe. The place is humming with hormones, and once they get it figured that pregnancy and STDs are a thing of the past, it's open season on any guy they fancy. And the guys? Well they're mostly on a Brad Pitt kick with a few hip-hop refugees thrown in. And don't forget the jocks – plenty of brain-dead drunk drivers here. Went to a field party and never came back. They're kinda preppy with muscles and still trying to get in your pants – yours and everyone else's. Some of them got *Boner Club* t-shirts and they grin at you like they're the greatest lay since Krishna.

7. The Victim's Island

Maybe it's time to tell you about the victim's island. I'm gonna have to tell you sometime – might as well be now. Sonja took me there first – one of her projects – trying to educate me, I think. It was well after I got settled and adjusted, unhitched the denial and all that. She asked if maybe I'd like to flex my wings a bit. I'd been at a dance club party place for hours and was, I think, kinda miffed at not really feeling the groovy kind of exhaustion you used to feel after that type of work out. It's funny the things you miss from life. Imagine missing feeling exhausted – too weird.

Anyway, Sonja picked her time well 'cause I was up for something different – a challenge I guess. We did the instant switch routine, *moving laterally*, as Sonja said, instead of up or down a level. I was, like, *so* embarrassed I didn't know the word laterally, and my dad used to use it all the time. We appeared on a hillside overlooking a small lake. Well maybe not that small, but you could see all the way round it, so it looked small. In the middle an island, with a couple of old looking stone buildings peeking out from under large over handing trees. Sonja gave me the skinny as we tripped down the hillside. The place had been entirely set up as a kind of rest home for screwed-up young women, most of them murdered. I figured she meant raped and murdered. You usually get the two in one package, don't you? Long time before, it had been a monastery for those souls who were used to that kind of scene before they died, but the whole monks-and-nuns thing had been in decline for a while and it wasn't getting the use, so some bright spark figured a once-over to fit it out for traumatized chicks. They all had their own rooms and were free to do what they wanted, which mostly was wander about the woods behind the place and pick flowers and stare into space sadly. *Sounds like my kinda scene,* I said, joking, what did she want me to do? Well, turns out she wants me to hang with them and help them get through their shit. *Oh, like a counselor,* says I, thinking great, fucked up teenies twitching an' bitching; mall rats from trashy families with attitudes to match; faces pasty from doughnuts and french fries. *Yeah sure, Sonja, whatever.* Course she picks up on that and ask me if I'd rather go back – I don't *have* to do it. Yeah, like I'm gonna back down now.

At the lakeside, we sit and feel the breeze on our faces. So nice I felt like lying down for a nap. So we did. I thought about Eric as I drifted off. We'd finally fucked a couple of nights before, at least nights for him, and it had been awesome. I wondered if he remembered in the morning. When you've been friends as long as we have, fucking is a whole different thing; It means more, and not just for Eric, who I think was a virgin, through he swears he and Cassie had a thing going before she left for the coast. For me too, despite all my history; let's face it, there's fucking and there's making love, and they're, like, two different things. And because it went so well and made us both so happy, I guess I'm like in love – almost. And that brings up all kinds of issues I'd rather not think about now. So I sit up and say *Yo! Let's go!* to Sonja.

Straight up Sonja says, *Wanna walk on the water?* Silly me figures there's a rowboat or something, maybe even a bridge somewhere. *Sure why not,* says me, figuring it's some kinda trick. I'm not religious, not really, but even I know only Jesus did that. Well, turns out anyone can – anyone that wants to. We did. Big fun too, once you get the hang of not letting your brain sink you. See, your brain is filled with all this… gunk that tells you what you can't ever do. Well, that was then, this is now. And now you can do just about anything you turn your mind too – if you've got a mind to turn that is. I'd done the flying thing already, most of the kids do, a couple of times at least, before they decide it's not cool or just too weird, but the walking on water thing, well, I'd never heard of it, or seen it done. Sonja says they keep it under wraps most of the time in case people get offended. I guess it's like you're making fun of Jesus or something – maybe

Mohammed too; did he walk on water as well? There's a girl down the hall from me who's got a Koran in her room. Maybe she knows. I'll stop in and ask her. That's another thing here that maybe you should know; everywhere there's people reading religious books trying to see where it fits their life. One guy said to me, we were sprawled on a lawn by a fountain (gees there's a lot of fountains here), *The Bible never tells you how much fun it's gonna be. And neither,* he said, *did the pastor.* I told him he musta went to the wrong church, that he shoulda gone to the everlasting church of fun like I did. He believed me for about ten seconds and then slapped my shoulder.

Anyway, getting way off track here. We walk over to the island with Sonja singing. She gets like that sometimes, says she's so happy she just has to. Those old Lovin' Spoonful songs, *Daydream* and *Rain on the Roof,* are two of her faves. Weird 'cause my mom usta like 'em too. She said sorry when I told her, but I said no problem, it reminded me of when she was happy and that was good. Lovely gardens about the place, beautiful overhanging willow trees, like a country estate. Wouldn't have minded living there myself. *That can probably be arranged,* Sonja said. Then she whispered, *See that one on the bench, head in a book, she was found all cut up in a dumpster.*

I looked at her, *You mean…?*

Yeah, the whole nine yards, abused, chained, starved. We got closer and Sonja called *Hi Cathy, how's it going*? Chick looked up for a second, gave us that waif stare and went back to her book. I know I'm supposed to have more sympathy for someone like that, but that stare-through-you-as-though-you're-not-there gaze, I've just had one too many chicks pull that one, usually 'cause they're doin' a number on you, and I just don't like it. Usually they just need to get a life, and I usually let them know.

Sonja said to come round the back and see some others, so we walked along one side of the building, past some carefully tended flower beds to this garden area at the back, with benches and deck chairs and some tables like you see in cafes. Couple of girls were sipping at drinks and working on their nails; they looked up and said *Oh hi Sonja* at the same time. We sat down and Sonja introduced me to Gail and Zoe. Zoe said something about hating her name and changing it and then we slipped into some regular girltalk that had me bored in no time. Sonja made an excuse and we stood up and said *See ya*! We were about to go inside when Sonja said, *No wait, there's something else I want you to see,* and she took me round the other side somewhere to this walled garden thing that she called a cloister walk. It was like all stone and archways and big gaps to see into the garden, which had like rocks and bushes and stuff. We strolled around it a couple of times, real slowly like it was a ritual. It was really quiet there, like someone had cast a spell on the place. Sonja said, *Not quite,* but that years and years of dead monks walking around in silent contemplation had created a calm so deep and thick we could still feel it. I chuckled when she said dead monks; I mean we're all dead here, but after a bit it's so hard to remember 'cause life just keeps goin' on and on like it never stopped, even though it did, in a way.

We slipped inside a side door that just appeared out of nowhere and somewhere I could hear laughter. It was a relief, that laughter, 'cause I thought we were gonna be stuck with a lot of poor-me losers. School had been full of them, most of them rich whiners, and I'd had my fill. After Sonja showed me about the place and I'd met up with a bunch of them, I could see they were different. If anything, they were trying a little too hard to have fun. It was pretty obvious from what Sonja whispered to me from time to time that they were all victims of violence and traumatized to the max. Some of them just stayed in their rooms and only came out for meals.

I wondered, after we left, how many of them thought that I was the same, especially coming in with Sonja like I did. I couldn't figure it then, but later I was to get a pretty good idea.

That first time though, I thought, why me? I don't need this shit. I got my family and Eric to cope with, that's tough enough. What did I need those silly bitches for? Not my fault they got murdered or raped and cut up. I mean, talk about fates worse than death – chain-sawed and chucked into sacks. Yuck! But still – me?

Sonja didn't push it. She just said maybe I, being nearly the same age and with a much better attitude, could help them adjust back to a more normal life. Course the concept of a more normal life here is a lot to swallow. What's normal? We're all dead for starters. Sonja acts like she knows what normal is, but though she's nice and all and been a good friend to me, well a teacher/guide kinda friend, I don't know that she knows, not really. She's like what people on earth would call stable and reliable, my parents sure would anyway, but her idea of what these girls should be doing, well, I dunno. And what ideas do I have? you're asking. Well I guess I'm still at the girls-just-wanna-have-fun stage. I know, it's sad, but there you go.

Like I said, Sonja didn't push it, she just dropped me off at my place and split (to see her boyfriend I think). I took a nap and then went down to one of my favorite hangouts; chillin' with my new best friends – all of us dead. *Dead with the grievers downstairs,* as Clint says; that's good enough for a t-shirt if you ask me – beats *Boner Club* any day. Clint arrived by way of some bad E – danced till he died. His buddy Kevin took it on the chin from some bouncer at the same club six months later. *Straight forward punch,* he says, *no problem,* but someone else kicked him in the side of the head while he was down and some kinda blood vessel broke and he was gone. The two chicks they've hooked up with, Sara and Megan, met in their first year at college and couldn't believe their luck when they died in the same car crash, drunk as skunks. Both of them had skipped so many classes they were sure to fail anyway. None of them seem very, like, sad, about dying, or missing their folks. It could be an act, I suppose, but maybe dying in the full flush of youthful rebellion makes you feel like you've triumphed over your adversaries, and you're cocky and couldn't-give-a-shit. Okay, I admit it, that was Sonja's line, but it's good, huh? I don't feel like I triumphed over anything really, I kinda miss the challenge actually, but I feel so sorry for Eric, stuck in that crippled body most of the time, that my shit feels like no shit at all.

So I tell these guys about the island. They're like, *Oh yeah? That's interesting. How fucked up are they? Like who gives a shit? We're dead, they're dead, get over it.* I thought, right, no compassion here, but you know that's no worse than me. I didn't want to feel sorry either. It's like you're on vacation here and no one wants to spoil the fun. Later, Sara said maybe she'd like to check it out sometime. I said *sure*. But she never did come. Neither did Sonja. Guess she figured I'd go by myself. And she was right. A couple of so-called days later (but there's no days here, we just kinda tumble helplessly into every next minute like puppies playing on the lawn), I went back to the island – *thought* myself there, like Sonja told me to; it's a breeze once you get the idea. Walkin' across that water sure was fun. I just told myself I could do it, and whammo, I was. There was a chick lying on the lawn flippin' through a magazine. I said *Mind if I join you*? She said *Nope* and patted the grass beside her. Then she says, *It's okay I know I'm dead, I got it all figured out*. I smiled and told her that was the worst part over, and now she could really get down and have some fun. I don't know where those words came from, I hadn't planned anything really, just felt I wanted to go. She said, *Fun, what's that*? I laughed, thinkin' Oh yeah, cute. Turns out she'd been held captive in some farmhouse basement by her foster parents for years, in a fuckin' cage if you can believe it, and starved to death. And, you know what, they got away with it; sold the property, buried her real deep, and moved outta state. She watched them do the whole thing, and hadn't a clue how to stop them or anything. Her guide finally got her attention, after like months, and brought her here. She taught herself to read from the old movie magazines that were tossed into her cage with the scraps of food. It was a movie mag she was looking at when I got there. But it was up to date, and since she hadn't seen anything past 1960, she was lost. She asked me about Audrey Hepburn. I told her there was a movie place where I lived where they showed old movies all the time, and I knew for a fact they'd shown Audrey Hepburn's 'cause I snuck in to see them myself. Had to, none of my new buddies would've approved. I was like an old film junkie back on earth; had all the Marlene Dietrich, all the Bogart/Bacall, a few Ingrid Bergman, oh the list goes on and on.

Lisa, that was her name, asks if she could come and see one. Then she says, *I dunno if I'm allowed to leave.* I said *Well, let's ask.* So we look around for someone in charge. A couple of the others look kinda clueless when I ask and shrug, like who cares? Another says, like real certain, *You gotta ask Marian and she's upstairs.* Like upstairs was some secret place no one could go. Lisa's already getting antsy, like she's sure the shit's gonna hit the fan. We meet this woman on the way upstairs and I say, *Are you Marian,'cause I'm a friend of Sonja's and I want to take Lisa to an Audrey Hepburn film.* Marian gives me a big smile and says, *Sure that'll be just fine.* Then she turns to Lisa and says, *You all have fun now.* Then Lisa starts crying. Turns out she can't believe people are being so nice to her. She's so sweet and innocent I feel like crying myself.

I'm thinking that if she's this weird about normal stuff, what's she gonna be like walking on the water. Marian, maybe she picked upon my thought, said, *Why don't you take the little powerboat, no one's using it right now.* Then she shows me where to find it. It's on the other side of the little island, moored by a cute little floating dock that was so sweet I thought Lisa was gonna start crying again. But she held it back this time and we hopped in, least I did and then helped her. It was one of those automatic glider ones, with the computerized directional thingee. You just think where you want to go and it goes there. Plus, it's got these little invisible beams it shoots out that tells it if another boat is coming anywhere close. I know because they got them where I live, which I guess I should tell you more about sometime. Lisa said she'd never been on one before, that she'd never left the island since getting there. A guide had brought her, the same guide that had watched her since she died and had been trying to get her attention for who knows how long.

I know I'm from somewhere else, she said outta nowhere.

Oh yeah, says I, *you know where?* I thought she meant Canada or France or something. *My people are strange looking, not like us.*

I thought, *Ugh, a nut, just my luck,* but then said, *You mean like on Star Trek*? Of course she hadn't seen that, or any TV at all I don't think. She didn't say any more about it all the time we were together. We did the instant transfer thing and suddenly we're looking at my little town place and she's saying, *Are we going there now*?

My little town: it's like a college town set way back in the hills, with all the stuff that little towns have and none of the shit that big towns have. I live in a dorm with lots of other kids my age. It's built, like totally funky, all curves and crazy glass. I mean glass that changes color with, I dunno, the time of day or something. You can see through it okay, but it glows like silvery and indigo and sparkles when you're kind of at an angle – really cool anyway. Classes are always available, but like totally optional. And it's not just screwing around either – we're talking serious work here. I'm thinking of American Lit and Intro to World Folk Music; I have to wait for them to start up again, but I sit in on some stuff now, just to get the feel of it. Course there's student pubs and clubs, and that's where most of the action is. At first you think it's just one big party college, but later you see quite a few digging into their course work. They're usually the ones who've been here a while and have overdosed on fun. That hasn't happened to me yet, but I'm guessing it won't be long. I wasn't so much like, studious before, but really interested in some stuff. It's just the stuff I was into they weren't teaching. A lot of kids weren't into anything except clothes and sex and partying, but I was into my own shit as well, but kind of off on my own mostly.

They weren't showing that Hepburn anytime soon, but the manager chick is kind of a friend of mine 'cause I'm like really into it and she digs that, and she said, *Look we got a little screening room for artsy shit and old stuff off to the side here, why don't the two of you watch it there?* I was like seriously impressed and said *Sure!* and Lisa was like totally amazed and followed me in like a disciple. Lisa would've been amazed to see the film at all, but to get her own private showing, well that was too much. She squeezed my arm and said thank you with such a glow in her eyes I coulda cried again. My little Lisa. I thought maybe I should adopt her.

Sonja had said something about adoption being a real option here, but I couldn't remember exactly what she meant, but I think it was more like, babies, you know, dead babies. See? Even the term makes you squirm. Dead babies, yucko! Like something some grotty punk band would put on their CD cover. But that's what they are, dead babies. But they look just fine, according to Sonja, that is; I haven't seen any – yet.

In a way I did adopt Lisa, doing my big sister thing, with that film as the first date. There's way more to tell, but I'll get back to it later. I want to move on to something else now. I get bored quick – even here.

8. God Hides

When I first got here I spent all of my time learning the ropes and trying to fit in. Then, once I'd found my niche, I set about having a good old time, which is like, so easy here, all you have to do is fall out the door and get going. And with plenty of people my own age with the same idea, everything just seems to roll along no problem. Sure there are the grievers to cope with, but you get the hang of that eventually – least most of us do; some seem permanently bummed out. You see them sitting off by themselves somewhere, head in a book, or gazing at the swans on the lake. Now I love reading, always have, and still do when I got the time, but there's reading and there's having your head stuck in a book – one's exploring and the other's hiding. I've met up with a couple and they're always, like, drowning in the sadness of their families. You try to tell them to, like, get happy and make the best of it but they just can't, or don't want to. They think hanging around the family weeping and moping along with them somehow helps; like it's the caring way to go; like you're a selfish shit for having a good time. That's when I see red, when I get that. I tell them they're full of shit and take off. I don't need that crap.

Anyway, that kind of leads me to the God thing. After a while you can tell that people are kinda wondering, like, if we're in heaven, where's God? I wasn't really concerned myself, but I'd notice people talking about it here and there. Clint says just because we know for sure there's an afterlife it doesn't mean God's alive and well. As he says, *It don't prove shit.* But you can run into kids that'll say just the opposite: *We're-dead-and-we're-here-so-there-must-be-a-God* kind of thing. They often turn out to be church kids that don't bother going now that their parents aren't around to check up, but who are still into the way the bible lays it down. I figure they really need to believe that there's a God; that they can't survive without that kinda comfort. Still, they might be right. I just wonder why they have this need to be right. So what if there isn't ? We're already in paradise, so what is there to worry about? Sometimes I wonder if they want something to worry about, like they used to worry about what their friends would think, about their favorite guy of the moment ditching them, about their father dying and leaving them no money for college, about not getting the prom dress they wanted.

Not that I didn't worry myself. I had all the usual teen girl hang-ups, and a few extras, all of my own devising. But I don't much now, except maybe my mother, and Eric – Eric the most, of course. My mother's got her boys, trash heaps that they are. This God thing though, why it gets people in knots is beyond me. Sonja says the exhilaration of paradise will keep me going for quite a while. She looked so smug when she said it, I asked if she'd seen God anywheres lately. She laughed and said, *Not likely, not on this plane anyway.* She keeps talking about planes. All I get is that there's different places with different kinds of people in them. And that's just like Earth.

The way I figure it, God hides. Course the next thing is, where? Not here, that's for sure. Sonja's got this thing where he hides in random acts of kindness, which is cool I guess, but isn't that more like what they call an attribute? Not the being, the almighty father dude on high. But I no more suspect some old guy in a chair than you do. Not even when I was nineteen and not much more than a walking attitude on drugs. Sure, now that I'm dead I'm the all-wise Melanie. If I was alive I might be twenty-one or so, but it's rougher to keep track of time up here. Why do I say *up*? 'Cause it feels like *up*. A step up, you know? But that's my story and I'm sticking to it – God hides. Why? So we'll look for him – look and keep looking; the light at the end of the tunnel; the present in the wrapping. It's the excitement of the mystery. We need it, else we'd die of boredom. Even here, where dying doesn't really matter.

Now Jesus seems to be just as much of a mystery, for the

former church goers anyway, some of who still go here - oh yeah, there's churches – all kinds – mosques and synagogues too. Like, not right here where I live but not too far away. Sonja showed me one time when I asked. I'd been talking to a church type and wondered if they were ever going to meet up with Jesus like they wanted to. She said that he's around and visits congregations by surprise, just walking in and sitting down and not saying who he is. She's not a practicing Christian herself but has heard he wants to test the quality of faith in every place he visits. Course she had to tell me why. Not being one of them I couldn't get the reason. He wants to see if the teachings are being followed. Like, are they really loving their neighbor? Do they live in the spirit of charity and mercy? Do they yearn for a state of grace with all their hearts?

Who has she heard this from? I asked. Oh, her teacher apparently; a teacher who's too remote for me to see as yet. Way up there I guess.

Is her teacher a Christian saint or something?

No, she says, *just someone who has evolved beyond the need for incarnation.*

Someone really wise? I asked.

Oh yeah, big time wise. Like an encyclopedia and a guru all mixed together, she said laughing. I notice that about Sonja, and her boyfriend, the little that I see him; just when you're getting into some really serious stuff, they break out laughing, like the whole thing – life, death, sports, society, music, whatever – is just one big joke. I guess I must look kinda pained or something 'cause she usually apologizes. I asked them if they were old hippie stoners, 'cause they always laugh and giggle a lot. Least the few I met did. You'd meet them buying pot 'cause they often had the best hydroponic around. So good even my dad slipped me some toke money. *Shit babe,* he'd say, *please don't tell your mother, she'll flip*. I think he smoked it on his weekends away with the boys. He must've 'cause there was never any left when I tried to mooch some. Anyway they're not. Sonja says she never smoked in her life. That life, the one before. She was a runner, hiker and skier, taught grade school somewhere in Canada and got eaten by a cougar somewhere in the Rockies. Died on, like, the second bite, she says – hardly felt a thing. And being a mountain lover, she felt she was intruding on the cougar's territory and deserved it for her stupidity. Wasn't even pissed at all. Just continued her cross-country ski. Went for days, maybe weeks, not knowing she was dead, wondering why she felt so awesome. Suddenly she was at her funeral, watching people weep. That was no fun. I know it.

Anyway I'm getting way off track. What was I talking about? Oh yeah, Jesus and all that. I guess I'd be kinda interested in seeing him – Mohammed and Buddha too. Just to see them for myself. I'm sure their religions are great and everything, but it'd just be neat to check 'em out up close, without all the hullabaloo that crowds would bring. Probably no chance though, I'm not even a believer. Why would they waste time on a little dead chick like me when they could be, like, inspiring thousands at a time?

I did see Kurt Cobain though, singing in a little club, with an acoustic guitar, just like that MTV unplugged show they did. Someone even asked for *Pennyroyal Tea*. I was kind of a fan, but way after he died. Not that many people know about him here. Not as many as you might think. Most of his fans are still alive see. Those seventies guys though, wow, they got a lot of fans here – been dead long enough I guess. Kurt seemed kinda shy, maybe even apologetic. He said he wasn't sure what to be singing about now that the afterlife was for real and all. Someone shouted *Sing anything we don't care*. He smiled and played some old blues song from like, the 1930's or something – something about God being a shining light in everyone's heart, nothing but a shining light. I liked that, even though it was a bit Sonja-ish.

Afterwards I asked him, backstage like – it was amazing no-one stuck around, I, like, had the place to myself – if he was pissed about... you know. Nah, he was, like – forgive and forget. Money and fame, it never was, like, a big thing for him. He lived for the music. Couldn't he, like, form another band here, since he missed his bandmates so much? Well he wasn't ready for that, see. He needed to get his bearings. He had a little place to live and was quite happy there, but he really had to rethink his attitude. This little gig was neat though, he'd really enjoyed it. He asked me what I was up to. I told him not much, which wasn't really true, but my life seemed already more interesting than his, and I didn't wanna upset him. But I did tell him about Eric, and the whole shitty situation with him being crippled and all, and me as free as a bird. It must've really gotten to him, so he asked if he could come with me and visit when Eric was asleep. I said sure, Eric would be, like, amazed.

I felt like I should ask Sonja for permission. What a wuss! Visiting Eric was something I did a lot by then, so why not just take Kurt along? So we arranged to telepath the whole thing. That's just like where you arrange with someone to send a thought when you're ready to do something and they, like, home in on your thought and they're there, standing in front of you. Everyone does it here. Well, you know, friends and stuff. It's way easier than phoning, or text messaging, which was just coming in when I died. Lotta things are easier here, but I think you know that already.

Eric was pretty amazed when we showed up. I came close first, just so he'd be, like, not freaked out, and then he was, you know, more at ease 'cause this out of body thing was still, like, amazing to him, and every time he'd be on the edge of *This can't be happening*, and I'd be like *Sure it is, it's me and I'm here*. So he's, like, *Oh man it is you!* and kind of falls into my arms. So when he settles down I tell him, *Hey Eric I got someone here to see you*, and Kurt, like, steps up, all smiles. The guys have a great little rap 'cause Eric was a fan for as long as I can remember. And I kinda just sit back and watch, like this proud mother hen. I started to see more and more ways I could make Eric's life better, even if it was only the asleep part. But what good would it do him if he couldn't remember? He'd said he was remembering bits and pieces during the day and wondering what it was all about. He'd told his mother and his best buddy Karl and they'd believed him, so that had helped. He also said it was weird the way meeting me here when he was asleep had, like, given him this double life. He could look at who he was in the daytime, and, like, see himself as another person. He didn't say anything about the obvious difference – crippled and not crippled – so I didn't either. Maybe I should have. But he seems to be coping well. I drop in unannounced during his daytime, and he's like doing stuff. Our old school is wheelchair accessible so he can take classes like before. He's like this History and Political Science pro and still whackin' out the projects. And it looks like being crippled will put him in line for colleges he wouldn't have had a sniff at before. And the chicks, he says, they're all over him. The sympathy vote, he calls it. Tell you the truth I'm jealous, but he says it's the same snobsluts he detested before. *The Heathers,* he says knowingly. That means Cindy and Dara and Heather. Heather even came by in her widow's weeds and after smarming his mom and arranging the flowers, offered to blow him. Understand, this is someone who would never cross the street to drag him from a burning building, never mind give him the time of day. Anyway, not knowing what else to do he went through the ordeal. *Just like a guy,* I said. But I forgave him when he said he spent most of it trying to piss in her mouth. Couldn't pull it off though, couldn't figure out how. Course I wanted to know if she swallowed. No, thank god, swiped it into a hanky – figures!

Anyway, the Kurt thing went well, and it sure gave me hope for the future – Eric's future that is. Kurt said later that it gave him hope too – hope that a useless piece of shit like him could actually help someone. I think he figures his death, with all its depressed suicide PR, caused a lot of shit for young people who looked up to him. He figures visits like this are a way to make up. And holy shit; he says he wants me to help him with it. I'm like seriously honored, but I really wanna talk to Sonja about it.

9. More Family Crap

Libraries, did I tell you about the libraries here yet? Wow, ever cool. I liked reading a lot when I was, like, alive, so I just kinda naturally drifted to the library here. The stuff they have you just wouldn't believe. Illustrated books? Yeah, but like a 3D pop up cartoon version? Screening rooms where you get to see a film about the author who wrote the book you're reading, including stuff about them as they were writing it, a film about Edgar Allan Poe with Edgar Allan staring in it! Just too cool! Machines where paragraphs, at the click of the mouse, turn into the action they're describing, TV's with the news from New York, Larry King and all that old folks crap. I don't know what it is, spy satellites or what, but we can pick up any TV or radio signal from Earth and play it here. Some folk are real interested and watch it, like, as if there's nothing else to do, all that soap opera shit too, girls still glued to that screen kiss, guys still groovin' to those blonde Baywatch babes.

Anyway, let's move on before I get too happy – wouldn't want that, would we; I might forget my duty to my grieving family. Dragged back into that house of horrors by my copiously weeping mother, I was doing duty by the sad bedside. I'd already tried holding her heaving shoulders and patting her softer-than-I'd-realized curls, neither of which put the slightest dent in her self-pity. There; I've said it finally. Not fair, you'll say – selfish teenager pissed that her parade's being rained on. Well maybe, but look at it this way: I've met up with her (with Sonja's help, early on when I didn't quite get the technique) when she was asleep, just like I do with Eric, and given her all the info she needs about my life now and she acts all happy and grateful, as if I'd come back from college for the weekend. So, the next time I drop in, she's back to wallowing in misery, usually in her bedroom, middle of the afternoon, sometimes with a side of wine, sometimes not, before the brothers return from whatever well-constructed lie they've engineered for the day. Then it's back to wrestling her out of sleep (yeah there's a technique for that too) and confronting her with the real me. I guess it sounds real impatient to be going on like this, but you have to see it from our point of view. One minute they're all happy and weepy and relieved and the next they're writhing in this swamp of suicidal self-pity. It's like the worst kind of bipolar going. Come to think of it, I'm not exactly sure what bipolar means, but I bet you do.

Maybe it's my payback for all that thirteen year old crap I put her through. I'll have to be honest, I was hormone crazy there for a while; ran away twice; stole her money and jumped on a Greyhound; lied about going to see an aunt in Boston when the ticket guy asked; wandered around, then took a cab to Faneuil Hall, 'cause I'd read about it in the New York Times magazine and started snacking. Guess my maturity act worked for a bit, 'cause they didn't suss me out till nighttime, when a cop found me sleeping on a bench; said I was lucky not to be raped or murdered; took me in and made me call home.

Anyways, there I am, helpless again as my mother rolls about in agony. I'm like *Oh shit what can I do?* almost in agony myself. Somebody taps me on the shoulder – I turn around – someone who looked a lot like Audrey Hepburn in the opening scene of *Breakfast*, the hair, the dress, the works – smiled at me and said *Why don't you try your father's secretary? She can see you*. I asked if she was Audrey or an angel dressed up as Audrey. I was so excited I was nearly jumping out of my skin. Audrey's like my all-time heroine. Stupid as it sounds now I tried like hell to be this Goth version of her, all dark poise and dry humor. But she was neither Audrey nor an angel; she was just a guide who figured doing the Breakfast thing would get my attention. I asked if she was a friend of Sonja's. She knew her, yes, but not really a friend – a colleague perhaps.

So we leave my mom washing her face in the bathroom and go

looking for Andrea. Well Andrea's doing her thing at work, I could've told her that, but what the heck! maybe she knew something I didn't. But as we were hovering there, watching Andrea type up something from a tape, I thought what does she know? Then, like it's a cue from the wings, she looks at her watch and begins to put things away and get ready to leave. I look at 'Audrey' and she winks at me. Nobody seems surprised to see Andrea leaving the office and she nods and smiles at everyone as she passes by. She walks a few blocks, like she's in no hurry to get anyplace fast, and then into a restaurant – kind of an upscale diner place, nothing too fancy. She joins my dad at a table, and I'd have to say, they seem pretty happy together. What's that they say; smiles light up their faces? Well it's true. There was a kind if glimmery light about them. Course, when you're a ghost, like I am, everyone has some kind of glow. But when people are in love they have a starry twinkle to them. And those two sure did. I didn't know whether to be envious or annoyed. Audrey draped her arm about my shoulders and whispered *Have mercy on them they're only adults.*

That worked. Calling them adults made them look like children. Don't ask me how, it just did. I already saw my mom as a child, so this was easier somehow. Part of me wanted to defend Mom, to shout *How dare you at a time like this?* but another part just kind of watched and wondered where it was all going to lead. Not back to her apartment, as you might expect, but to a couple of drinks, some nachos with cheese and hot peppers, and some smiles and shared laughs. Oh, and a hug and a kiss when they parted outside – very sweet, just like romantic lovers. I figured we'd be following Andrea home and we did. Audrey, still in her amazing Breakfast outfit, asked if I wanted to high tail it to the apartment and wait or follow along. She looked as if following along was going to be more fun, don't know why, so I said *Let's follow.*

Sure enough she had something up her sleeve: she showed

me how to walk through people, basically by saying *Hey check this out*, and walking through a big burly guy like he wasn't there. Course, it's us that aren't there – aren't there to them, the real people. I was watching, and she just disappeared into him, for the shortest of seconds, and then was there on the other side, grinning. Then I tried it. We were down at sidewalk level, so there was plenty opportunity. I picked a woman with a bundle of shopping bags (not a bag lady, a lady with bags) Shopaholic city – shoot it was easy. She felt like, I dunno… sand, grated cheese, some kinda texture like that; like thick air, if there is such a thing. And I sorta popped out the other side. I howled, Audrey grinned. It was so much fun I did it again – a guy in some weird outfit, then a knot of teens waiting to cross. That was even more fun, in and out, in and out.

Audrey then surprised me by walking into the wall of a building. She just disappeared. I knew it was a challenge, just as if she'd thrown down a gauntlet, so I walked in behind her. Not thick air this time, just thick. Stuff packed more closely together. Kinda panicked in the middle there, thought I was going to get stuck, but a hand appeared and pulled at me and I was through. Audrey, of course; she'd sussed out that I was having trouble. *I'm a guide*, she smirked, *I know everything*.

We were in a big department store, so we wandered about, checking out clothes and jewelry – nice stuff too, although we got lots of nice stuff where I live now.

So we get to Andrea's place, and it's a bit like before, except she does a few chores first. When she sits down to meditate, we know it won't be long. Sure enough she comes floating up out of her body and sees us. I'm about to introduce Audrey but Andrea gets the outfit right away and says *Breakfast at Tiffany's, right?* Little bit of chit-chat and then I tell her about Mom and can she do something, anything, get it across so that she won't be so down all the time. She says she'll try, but that her memories when in the body are, like, really vague. Like she knows I'm okay, but not really enough detail about why and where to convince anyone. She's tried it with my dad a few times, and he's like, he wants to believe, but keeps having all these nagging doubts. When I try him at night, he never seems to come out of his body at all. Sonja says some people are just like that. Some float up out of their body but still stay asleep, just three feet above, *doing the hover*, as she calls it.

Audrey suggests to Andrea that we do something a little wacky so that she'll remember it. She thinks that sounds like fun, and so do I, but then we get into this thing, like, okay what? and we stand about like none of us have ever had an idea before. Finally Audrey says *Why don't you dance with her?* Andrea says, *Great, lets make some costumes.* Then she looks at me and says *You wanna be the guy*? As I'm thinkin' that one over she's suddenly like this ante-bellum southern belle from Charleston or Savannah, so I gotta be this Confederate captain guy. I can't get all the details of the uniform right so Audrey helps me. At the last minute we shrink my hair to the right level and Audrey whips out a mirror for me. Amazing – like me in a uniform. I start singing that old Gang of Four song *I Love A Man In Uniform* (way before my time but Eric's, like, connected to some serious collector types and gets burns of all this great old shit) – and twirling about – chuckles all round. Andrea's really done a number: a giant fuscia flouncy billowy thing and lustrous black hair with a big-time design job that would've taken hours to style in its day. That's the neat thing about here, you can imagine stuff and want it and then it's there – or mostly there. I had this half-assed idea of a Confederate uniform so a half-assed uniform was what I got until Audrey sorted it out.

So we begin this pretty good fake waltzing about to this old-timey waltz music that I bet Audrey whipped up out of nowhere. Guides are like that, they know all the tricks. It was fun, twirling around gracefully. Andrea did the leading, she obviously knew the steps. I'd just seen it done in movies and kinda went with the flow. It was neat being a guy for a while, but at the end, I had this inspiration. I suddenly turned into my old Gothgirl outfit and stuck my tongue out. Andrea broke out of her refined southern belle thing and squealed. I was proud of my little contribution and took a bow, and then remembering who I looked like, a curtsy. Mega applause.

Andrea says something about her meditation ending and says *au revoir* with a grin. We watch her settle back into her body. An almost imperceptible shiver and her eyes open. She yawns and shakes her head. Our job is done, I don't know what we're watching for. Then Andrea stands up and walks over to a table and picks up a notebook and pen and starts to scribble. Audrey smiles and nods as if to say *See!* Five minutes later she's checking a number and dialing. Oh my god, she's talkin' to my mom! She apologizes for disturbing her at supper time and says she just had to tell her about this dream she had about me. Dancing with me around and around, except I was dressed as a soldier, but at the end I suddenly became my old self and started laughing. Audrey looks at me and says, *Let's go check it out*. She grabs my hand and we reappear at my house. Mom's holding the phone and staring out the kitchen window into the back yard and saying stuff like, *How can you be so sure*? I think, to her, this is dad's secretary telling her she has had a dream about me. Dad's secretary who's only met me, like, about twice. She's thinking, why would I appear to Andrea in a dream, and not her? I shout, like so impatient, just like I always was with her, *Mom I come to you all the time but you don't remember! Get a life!* Of course it does no good, she can't hear me, but Audrey does, and she shushes me like, *There's no point, calm down!*

She's right, I know from a hundred times before. You can stomp and shout and wail but living people just don't get it. They're grievers, like my buddy Clint says, and they want their version of what's happened, they don't want yours. *It's like they don't want you to be happy*, he says, *they want you to be all fucked up and miserable like they are,* and I'll tell you there's times when I agree with him.

So my mom thanks Andrea for taking the time to call and says goodbye. Then she walks up to my dad's study, where he's going over some papers or something, and tells him the story. His eyes widen and he says, *What do you think? Sounds like Major Mel, no?* My mom grins and says, *Yeah it sure does,* turns around and walks away. Then calls *Dinner's nearly ready,* when she's going down the stairs past the boys' bedroom so they'll hear too.

I look at Audrey and say, *Thanks for all your help.* She smiles, still in her Breakfast outfit, and says, *Sure no problem, love to help when I can. You goin' back to your place*? I say, *Yeah I guess, not much more to do here I suppose.* She blows me a kiss. *Okay then see ya!* And she's like, poof, gone. Guides are so fucking cool I tell ya.

10. Some Fun Stuff

So do you see the kinda crap us dead kids have to take, even though we're in paradise? Some have got it worse than me, way worse. I'm just kinda like your average American with a family of fuck-ups. At least no one's in jail, but the way Gran's going with her peace activist stuff that could change lickety-split. She thinks being seventy-five gives her the right to shout and cuss at cops and call down politicians. The other three grandparents are here, and they do not approve, but I'll get to that later. This is time for some fun stuff – for me and for you.

With its college-party town atmosphere, my neighborhood has more than its fair share of fliers. It's the kind of crazy fun thing that kids just love – makes motorbikes and bungee jumping look pathetic. The buzz is incredible. The buzz in just being here, in deadworld, is pretty awesome to begin with, like you're all bubbly and energetic without the java, or any kind of drug really, but flying is like the buzz times ten, maybe times a hundred. Most just can't get enough of it. Even kids with serious thrill issues warm up eventually.

When you first get here from the scene of the death, like I did, with a guide, it's the automatic transfer method. At least that's what Sonja did and she says everyone just about does the same – gets you to close your eyes and hold hands. Then they just decide to move a level or dimension or whatever. For them, with all their experience, it's just a click of the fingers and you're there. Well, here. Then they show you how to do it, 'cause they know you're going to feel the pull of the grievers and it's better you know how to switch under your own steam than be dragged about by their needs.

Sonja didn't actually tell me about flying, I found out for myself. After what I guess was a couple of days (it's so hard to figure time here, not that I gave much of a shit before, but at least you went to sleep and woke up in the morning), I was walking down by the lake, just kinda grooving to the swans and the little sailboats, when I see these kids flying over the water, low, like just above the surface – skimming, I guess you'd call it. *Wow!* I thought, *that looks pretty cool.* Deadworld had shown me a few tricks by then, and I was on the lookout for more, but this was something else. I strolled over to the water's edge to see if I could get their attention. I couldn't figure out why they weren't drawing a huge crowd. Best I describe it was like they were imitating seagulls. In fact, when I got to talk with them, that's pretty much what they said.

They asked if I was new here – like it wasn't pretty obvious – then one of them took me aside and showed me the basics, starting with just lifting off the ground in the stand up position – a few feet to begin with. I was a bit wobbly at first, nerves I guess, like riding a bike for the first time. There's no need to flap your arms, but you wanna do it anyway. All those bird fantasies you had as a kid I guess. There's the excitement and then there's the fear, so you plop back down again. Fear of what? Falling I guess. It's all that earth stuff that you can't forget. Eventually you do, but at first it's as fresh as a fist in the face, which as you may know is quite the chick thing these days. I got slapped by one of the Jennifers, a cruise team of bitches from school who took the football squad as their own, but that's another story. She said, from ten feet up and grinning, *Come on! You can do it!* So I tried again, no wimp me, and it worked a bit better. I stood my ground beside her like a champ.

Okay, so I learned the ropes. Not that interesting, really. Sure is fun to do though. You probably won't believe me till you get here. It's just too far out, isn't it? Even Eric has a hard time when we're sitting in his bedroom watching him sleep. It's like he can go so far but no further. And I don't suppose you believe you can go even that far. Dead people flying around like birds? Must be angels, right? Nah, just dead people. See, there's dead folk and there's angels – two different things. Angels are angels, you know, saintly and wonderful. The rest of us are just dead. Still as hung up on that same old shit and if not that then some new same old shit. Still and all we're here having some kind of life, maybe not the one you figure on though.

Now I can fly like a pro. Those training wheels are off. I can do all that stuff that you see those stunt flyers do at air shows. Not just me, lots of people. Usually we go a ways into the countryside. Not sure why, they were doing it when I joined. I guess the tradition had been established. Kinda unusually thoughtful for people our age, I thought. Sometimes though you'll see guys right in town on one of the main drags, just lift off for no reason, for fun. Usually that means they haven't been here that long and just can't resist. Mostly no one pays attention; it's no more unusual than someone skateboarding where you are.

Some of the streets are this squishy rubbery stuff that never wears or dents or anything and is so soft and easy to walk on, and others are this lovely grassy stuff that is amazing on your bare feet, though lots of people, fashion slaves mostly, still wear trendy shoes. There's cars parked in garages and driveways but you hardly ever see anyone using them. Why drive if you can fly? Not to mention flip over to Africa or India in a second. That instant transfer thing isn't just for coming from earth to deadworld here. You can use it to go anywhere – anywhere in your comfort zone I guess I should add. Sonja's told me there's places I wouldn't be comfortable in. *Vibrations too high,* she says. Course that brings out the rebel in you, least me. So she took me. Man was it bright! Like seriously intense. Uncomfortably white hot, like inches from huge floodlights. Couldn't handle it. Said to Sonja *Get me outta here!* Don't even know where it was. Course the whole idea of *where* is a new ball game here. There's gotta be maps and stuff, but I ain't seen them yet. Guess all I have to do is ask, but you can't think of everything. This here's a new world, and nothing's quite as you first figure it, if you figure it at all.

Sonja'll answer any question I can think of, but sometimes you just get tired of asking.

Another fun thing is swimming underwater. You can go for ages, no need to breathe. That's right – no need to breathe. Sure, everyone breathes, it's natural. How could you not? Well here you don't have to, though it can takes ages to get the message. Sonja said, *We don't like to tell people right away as it's so close to their normal way of functioning they can't imagine existence without it. They think they need to breathe, like they think they need to eat and sleep, but it's better if they find out in their own good time.* Or something like that. I still do all three, but the swimming underwater showed me I didn't really *need* to breathe. You start out holding your breath like you're told to, and you're kinda tense like it means something, but you remember what you've been told, just relax babe, and suddenly the pressure, like, sags, and you're just groovin' along lookin' at the fish and whatnot. After the excitement of that dies down, then they tell you you don't really have to swim, you just have to think about where you wanna go. That takes a bit of getting used to, but after a while it's, like, natural. Guys tell me it's better than snorkeling, way better – so all you snorkeling dudes get ready for that. Course you may have to wait fifty years to get here, but there's not much I can do about that. I guess you'll just have to eat shit for a while, won't you? Sonja tells me I shouldn't take that attitude, that it's not constructive. Plus I don't wanna make kids off themselves just to get here. There's more than enough of them doing that now anyway, don't give them a good reason. She told me the figures for teen suicide once, but I forget. I know it was huge though – really shocked me, like figures for a war.

There's like, a lot of other stuff that's big fun too, like the feeling of no gravity or something. You feel light as a feather most of the time, like you could just float away on the breeze. And sometimes you do – only if you let yourself though. It's not like you actually *are* a feather. That lightness really makes dancing more fun too. You're like this total energy babe. Better than any E. There's lots that take E here. I tried it a couple of times, out of habit really, why say no, I mean you're dead what else can possibly happen, and thought I was smooth, but wasn't sure. I felt high, but there seemed to be no getting high. And certainly no come down. Although lots of others said they felt it. There's this big debate about whether drugs here make any difference. Some swear they do, and others, like me, aren't so sure. Sonja won't comment; says I have to make up my own mind, and then laughs. I like that about her. Though she's, like, really knowledgeable about things here, she doesn't shove it down my throat, she, like, gives me room to move, which is great 'cause the last thing I need is another mom, or more teachers. Now that's not to say I didn't like some of my teachers, a couple were cool; Barry Cannon for History and Media Studies and Ruth Wells for Lit and Language were both great, really cool, and I kinda miss them. They took my Goth girl freakishness and worked with it, rather than sneering at me like some did. I'd love to tell them both about the Afterlife here. I bet they'd be interested. Must talk to Sonja about that.

Other fun stuff? Well, sex of course, what did you think? That everything else was a blast and that was, like, a bore? I don't think so. It doesn't take long for people to find out that pregnancy isn't happening here and neither are STD's. Well three cheers for that I said. Aside from this recurring Clamydia shit I had going on earth, I kept getting these weird little pimply things that coulda been herpes but weren't. At least according to Emily, whose mom was a doctor and had all the literature at her house. Emily would like, consult, with the texts when someone was freaking. She was really cool about it. Some chicks would've wanted money. Others, of course, would just spread it around, letting everyone think you were HIV. One of the Jennifer's was positive I swear – never seen anyone with so many colds and flu and shit. And she did a lot of coke too. She was seeing this muscle man bouncer guy and I'm sure he was feeding her lines to get her hooked so he could put her out to trick for him. Everyone said I was racist 'cause he was black, but shit, it was obvious. *Use you goddamn eyes,* I'd say, *what does it look like to you?*

But they were all blind; couldn't see past his cool wannabe rapper shit to the pimp beneath. And I never did find out what happened – died too soon. I guess I could flip down soon and find out though. See, that's the thing about being here; there's so much to do and so much you can do and you just keep thinking of more and more. Sonja says, *Keep thinking Mel, that's my girl.* I know she's teasin' but sometimes I think she's only half teasin', like she's got plans for me. I guess I'll find out one way or the other.

Notice how I keep getting off track? That's me I guess, a featherbrain full of ideas, always shooting off in five directions at once. I'd apologize but I know it's not gonna get any better. You're gonna have to get used to it. So the sex stuff, back to that. It really is awesome. If you dig orgasms then this is the place for you. You can be with your soulmate or you can screw around. I kinda screwed around for a bit and then kinda focused on Eric. But if he didn't get out of his body at night I'd be stuck screwing around. Least I think I would. But there's people here doing both. Some say they found their soulmates and others just laugh and say who gives a shit. For them it's just one big party – March break for all eternity. And you know what, no-one tells them any different. Yeah they get rowdy, yeah they get noisy, but not for long. I think it's because there's nowhere near the pressure here. Oh, there's peer pressure to be cool and sharp, but there's no parental stuff and no exam career shit breathin' down your neck. And no fast food managers shittin' on you for being late and not trimmin' your hair, as one guy said to me. Another thing: nothing breaks here, not glass, not wood, not nothing. Took me while to notice that. And spills, they're no problem either – just wipe 'em away. Nothing seems to sink in – red wine, blood – it just kinda disappears. After a while you get used to it and don't think about it anymore. Sonja says that what you expect, happens. And that before you really expect anything, everyone else's expectations take over, like in social situations. *So, the first time I seen wine spilled, the reason it didn't stain was that some one else expected it not to?*

Pretty much, she said. *It's all to do with thoughts and how you think them.*

Sonja says *Mel if you can grasp that you've got it made*. I laughed and told her I'd think about it.

11. Wanna Tell Ya

Wanna tell ya about a wild trip Sonja took me on a while back. Just one more thing you find out you can do here. Sonja says the list is endless and I'm beginning to believe her. I'd been asking her about the Iraq war as I'd died just before *the awesome socks*, as Eric called it – still does actually. So Sonja says she doesn't give much of a shit about wars anymore, but that she can take me there if I want. I say, *Yeah like I really want to get munched or vaporized.*

Don't be a goof, she says, *you're already dead. They can't kill you again.*

You mean we're going in as ghosts?

Yeah, she says, *how else could we pull it off?*

So after a bit of minor league anxiety from me and some wimp ass talk from her, she puts this energy shield around me (don't ask! It's some kind of protection against fear and anger or something), gets me to close my eyes and suddenly we're there – in this dust storm kinda thing; like a January snowstorm except tiny bits of dust.

They have them in all those desert countries, she says. They've got a name, which, of course, I can't remember. Wow, weird. Couldn't see a thing, and couldn't figure why we landed there of all places. Couldn't we, like, see some action?

She tells me it's always like this. It's a dusty place to start with and the bombing just stirs it up even more. She tells me we're where the front was at yesterday, and it was ablaze with action then. Looks like we're in a street of some kind: I can see walls of dried mud or something and the road surface is like dirt, hard packed. As we move I see, like, trash lying around, old cans, paper, and broken bits of shit I just can't figure at all. A mangy dog kinda shivers by, like he thinks we're gonna kick him. He looks like he hasn't eaten in a month. I can hear cracking noises somewhere, like a whip or a firecracker or something. Then a man hurries by like we're not even there. He's got the traditional cloak type clothing but no beard like you think they would. Sonja says *He's dead. Can you see?*

I say *no, how am I supposed to tell?*

They're brighter and their feet don't always touch the ground.

Okay I'll watch for that, I say, not really getting the point. I look in a window we're passing. It's dark inside but I can just see what looks like a bundle on a bed – a bumpy bundle. A woman sits by the bed on a low wooden stool, her hair thrown back and her mouth open, like she's fallen asleep with her head against the wall. Sonja's beside me and responds to my thought: *Yeah, that'll be two or three kids under the blankets.*

Soldiers rush by, running and then squatting and then running again, looking up at rooftops and pointing their weapons. One of them hurries back, runs right into us, and I mean *into,* peers in the window like he's lookin' for trouble, mumbles and then rushes off. Sensation of him in me was like me in those others on the sidewalk. I felt sorta thick and heavy, like I was made of carpet, instead of air like I usually feel. I know that sounds weird, but there's a lot of shit here that you just can't describe. But I can describe how I felt about that woman with her head back – sadness, pity, love. I just wanted to run in there and grab 'em all and take them back to heaven with us. I just knew they'd never be happy here, wherever here was. Someplace in Iraq I guess. But Sonja jiggled my elbow and indicated we should be moving along. She guessed what I was feeling of course, but only spoke about it when we were back home safe. Not that you're not safe as a ghost in a war; nothing can get you – bullets, bombs, knives, whatever – but you don't feel right there, it's too fucked up. What she said was, *Mel, you can't just take people away from their hell, they have to want to go first.* Course when it's living people and you're a ghost, that's, like, obvious. They can't see or hear you, no matter what. But as life went on, life here that is, I saw that what she said was true here too. Oh, never mind, you'll see later.

Seconds later, another alley type street, more garbage and a couple of bodies, slumped, twisted, half burnt one of them. Awful; worse than one of those tacky horror flicks. Around the corner of a wall – a little square thing, like a big courtyard – a mess of dead bodies all close together, like a massacre or something, like they'd all been shot at the same time. I noticed that none of them had shoes or boots and knew right away that they had been stolen by whoever had shot them and that the whole thing was some kind of payback time. Sonja made me look at one corner of the yard. There was a huddle of guys, like, conferring. I wondered if they were dead. Sonja nodded and said, *Watch me for a minute.*

I was a bit freaked, but what could I do? She took a few steps towards them and her clothes, like, changed into Arab gear – you know, all that cloaky headdress stuff. She had her back to me but somehow I knew she turned herself into a guy. Not a sex change, but a looks change. She, like, catches the attention of these guys, and heads get bowed and a serious looking conversation goes on. I wait. I don't think they even see me. I look at the heap of bodies on the ground and then at the heads bowed in conversation. Amazing – the same people – the dead parts and the live parts. I hope you can understand this, 'cause it's like, really important. Sonja comes back to me, the guys watching but keeping their distance.

They didn't believe me, she said.

Believe what? I asked.

Believe that we're guides that can take them to heaven. Still, you can't blame them, been suspicious of every move for decades, habit they can't give up.

Oh yeah they know they're dead alright, she told me once we were out of the courtyard, *they just don't think I'm the right guy to lead them to heaven. Started asking questions from the Koran, course I couldn't answer them. They were looking for a proper Muslim guide, a Sunni one. Should never have worn that outfit, made me look like a spy.*

A little batch of Marines came rushing by, doing their look-and-point routine. We turned without talking to watch them, peeking around the wall into the courtyard. They examined the heap, poked their rifle butts into a couple of corpses, looked at each other and rushed off. The Iraqi ghosts looked relieved and smiled at one another. We turned and moved on. It was still all dusty and dim, but somehow I'd gotten used to it and could see a bit better. I wondered why we didn't go through some walls. Sonja heard my thought and said we'd be invading someone's privacy and that wasn't right, unless they'd been killed and we'd have a chance of retrieving them. I saw then that there were rules for what we were doing there, even in a war. I guess there was a Geneva Convention for ghosts too.

We came to some major street. It was wide and strewn with garbage, broken trucks and things on fire – things like army vehicles. Not tanks exactly, but big tough looking things, useless now that they'd been bombed. It was like walking onto the set of a war movie and everyone had quit for supper or something. Like that war movie Eric made me watch 'cause he was convinced it was like almost true. Umm, black something down… yeah, *Black Hawk Down*. You ever see that one? That's the one where we got our asses kicked in Africa; the one where they called us the paper tigers after. Least that's what Eric told me and he's really into that stuff – even now.

Sonja strolled about, like we were looking for a nice spot to have a picnic. I felt really weird. We'd been here a while and I'd felt not that bad, not that bad for a ghost I guess, but this busted-up bombed-out crap made me feel really strange. Don't know why. Feelings here are just like feelings there, lotta stuff that you just don't get. Sonja says she's looking for dead guys. There's some around, she just knows it. Ghosts looking for ghosts, don't ya just love it? Better than TV, I tell ya. She tells me we better start looking like Americans again, waves her hand and we're back to jeans and sweats and runners. I watch her lift off and float into one of the bombed out truck thingees – bigger than trucks though. She looks down at me, as if to say, coming in? With my thoughts, I say no thanks, I'll wait here, and in she goes. I look around, like I'm almost afraid – this little girl out on her own in a war. Like, as if I can get hurt or something. It's like the creepy feelings from earth follow you here. Like a bad habit I guess. I look around, spooked by my own stupidity.

Sonja reappears leading a couple of soldiers by the hand – all gored and burnt, seriously dead. Of course they're not dead really. I know that and you know that but they sure don't. She settles them down beside me and introduces us – Mark and Danny. Sonja tells them to wait with me as she goes ghost hunting. I'm like freaked, wondering what the hell I'm supposed to do. Do a Florence Nightingale I guess, but what's that all about when you're dead?

You another angel? This from the Danny one.

Me? Nah, I'm just dead, ordinary dead, nothing special about me.

Mark starts to cry and Danny hugs him. What about his kids back home in Wichita? He'll never see them again. Danny tells him, *It's okay man, we'll work something out.* I butt in all excited and tell them that going back to see your family's like so easy even I can do it, a dumb ass chick like me. They look at me, shocked I guess.

Danny says, *You serious?*

I say, *You bet. Get yourselves cleaned up and I'll take you. That's if Sonja doesn't have, like, other plans.* Then they want to know how they can get cleaned up around here. I tell them it's easy. All they have to do is imagine themselves free of all bruises, cuts and burns. Not to mention all the caked dirt and crap all over them. They looked kinda cynical, like Oh yeah really? I said, *Really. Just try it. Imagine yourselves all clean and nice and ready to do some visiting.* Neither of them seemed to have a clue how to go about it, but at least Mark had stopped sobbing, which was a relief. They looked at each other and then at me. I said, *Okay just try wishing you were neat and clean*. Mark's face was first, kinda fuzzy and then smooth. Then his hair went all neat and tidy. Danny laughed and slapped him and the back. Mark looked – what's that word? – nonplussed, you know, freaked. He looked at his arms and the burnt raggy cloth became clean and smooth. I shouted, *See I told ya!* Danny suddenly had his dress blues on, but his face needed work. I reminded him and the bloody bruised skin became, like freshly shaved and shiny.

Sonja reappears with more dead guys – about six in all. They all knew each other. The next thing I knew they're all teasing Danny for looking so sharp, like, where's the parade dude? There's this general hilarity for a bit, with Sonja and me watching on and eventually they're all in their blues, ready to move. Sonja wants to take them to a reception center place, like one where I went but more for soldiers, but since I'd already told Danny and Mark about visiting families there was some dissention in the ranks. I felt like I'd blown it, but Sonja said, *No, take them to their families and then we'll hook up later.*

And how exactly was I gonna do that? I asked quietly. Sonja made some joke about me being a trainee, and reminded me that all I ever had to do was think about being with her and I would be, and not to forget to bring the soldiers with me.

No sweat, she said. No sweat, my ass! I sweated the whole way. Taking Lisa from the Island to the movies for the day was a breeze compared to this. Man, I was aching to be partyin' somewhere, but here I was with a bunch of dead Marines in Iraq, two of whom I was taking to visit their families. We weren't in Kansas anymore, Toto, but we were just about to go back… with Major Mel as tour guide.

Remembering Sonja's basic instructions, I took the hands of both guys and had them close their eyes. Sonja said it was standard operating procedure and to just ignore their macho resistance. I executed the *Wichita, Kansas* intention and we were standing in a park somewhere, with the usual park stuff happening. Both guys were amazed. Holy shit here we are, kinda thing. Amazed, like kids who snuck into a carnival. A few minutes walking about, checking out their new ghost status. Making dumb faces at strangers. It was fun to see them having fun, especially Mark, who looked like he was headed for the psyche ward a while before. Eventually he came to me as Danny was chasing ducks on the pond, and asked about going to his family. Danny said he'd stay in the park till we got back.

I wasn't exactly sure what his family consisted of, but there'd be kids for sure, 'cause he'd already mentioned them. With a confidence I was, like, totally faking, I told him to hold my hand close his eyes and think of being home with his family. I was a bit nervous letting him lead, but it never occurred to me until later that I could have just made the move; I didn't actually have to know the family ahead of time. We opened our eyes to see a driveway and a car. A woman was helping two little kids get in. It looked to me like some after school trip to McDonalds or something; a boy and a girl, both really cute – maybe five or six. Mom looking a bit stressed, like she'd just come back from work and had twenty things to do before bedtime. I dunno, maybe I'm just revvin' it up. Mark just stood there staring for a bit. It was kinda sad really. I knew he'd be able to see them lots later, but maybe he didn't and figured this was goodbye or something. He watched his wife start the car and I said, *We can follow them if you want.*

He said, *Sure.*

So I took his hand and said, *Float with me.* He looked at me like I was weird so I said, *Mark we're ghosts we can float, we can go through stuff, we can even fly.* He looked like Oh yeah? I decide to float and off we went. We caught up to the car no problem and just kinda tailed it for a bit. It was fun! I think even Mark was digging it, even though that was his kids in the car, kids that couldn't see him.

I couldn't believe it; they turned into a McDonalds and parked. Amazing, me a prophet? Maybe that was another thing ghosts could do. I'd have to ask Sonja. We hovered, watching. The kids were excited and ran into the building while their mom locked the car doors and checked the trunk for something. The store had one of those like rubber rooms full of squishy balls and the two of them were jumping around in no time. Mom followed them in and went to the counter to order. We were standing behind her when I said, *Why don't you go in there with them and I'll wait here? Might be fun*. He grinned and turned to go. I sat with the mom as she munched on her meal and looked through some bills or mail or something. Like when I was in the hospital way back when, I got this real strong feeling for her thoughts. Lot of typical mom stuff I guess: the kids' clothes, some other kid on their street that was a bully, some friends having a party that weekend and what she might wear, and at the end, kinda, as if she was trying hard not to think it, some stuff about the war and Mark – worry stuff, you know. If I'd been sitting there with her I'd have said something nice and reassuring, but from where I was standing now, I wanted to sit her down and have a serious talk. It was too sad, what with her sitting there now sipping her coffee and staring happily, I thought anyway, at her bouncing kids. Course I was looking at their bouncing father, Mr Parade-Ready Marine, bouncing beside them, and what looked like through them too. At least he was laughing. Eventually the boy and girl came through looking for a Happy Meal.

I stood up before one of them sat on me. Mark was right there beaming. He thanked me for bringing him. He said that bouncing thing was about the most fun he'd had all year. I spent about three seconds wondering why he'd been able to bounce and not, like, go right through, and then made a note to ask Sonja. He said they'd spent a long time putzing about waiting for the government to make up its mind about the war, and then the fighting, so it had been ages since any of them had some R and R. He looked at his wife, well, longingly. More kind of sexual than sad, I thought, but of course I didn't ask. You know what, he looked like he wanted to drill a hole in their bed with her underneath him. I was afraid he'd like insist on trying to communicate somehow and wind up frustrated and angry, but he seemed to get the ghost thing right off, as if he'd been one before and knew the ropes. I know that sounds strange, but that's what I thought. He was way too comfortable with everything. I asked if he wanted me to go outside so he could be alone with them, and he said, *yeah, that would be nice.* So I floated out to the parking lot and just kinda hovered, watching everything going on. It was really relaxing. For a while I forgot I was dead and leading a couple of dead marines around as they made their fond farewells. It was neat just to be hanging there, seeing all the action, even if it was just the usual late afternoon suburban family routine.

I wished I could've done this kind of stuff when I was still on earth. It would have been so much fun. Sonja says I could've done it while out of my body at night, like Eric is now, but I kept *well inside the flesh,* as she says. I forgot to ask her how she knows that. Maybe it's just obvious. Right then I made a promise to myself. I'd show Eric all this stuff. So far he'd only made it to his bedroom and was happy enough with that. I was too; our bond had really, like, deepened. But I just had to get him out and flying about. It would be my gift to him.

Mark appeared down below, looking more or less like a Marine coming out of McDonalds. I could see he was wondering where I was, so I floated down towards him, coming in at a low angle. His reaction was funny: saluting me and smiling – pretty good when you think about what he must have just been through. We returned to the park and found Danny was missing. I thought, Oh shit, what am I gonna say to Sonja? Mark was sure we'd find him somewhere, so we began floating about the area, which I could see Mark was really digging. I had to admit it was a beautiful park and hovering our way around it was pure pleasure. I was just kind of hung-up on my tour guide responsibilities I guess.

Well the skinny is Danny finally showed up, a shit-eating grin on his face, and a brag about some beautiful chick. No, he didn't really want to drop in on his wife. Things had been lousy between them for a spell and his being away hadn't helped any. But he did wanna see his ma and pa. So off we went to some farm in Indiana. A lady in a kitchen chopping vegetables and talking on a cell, and a guy in a barn doing, you know, stuff. Danny looked lovingly at them both and we kinda wander about the property a bit. Danny went into some woods nearby to look at some childhood thing while Mark and I waited, respectful, without knowing why. Then he said he was done and we could go. I got them to hold my hands, close their eyes, while I thought intensely of Sonja. I think I was even gritting my teeth. Course, I hadn't a clue where she was but suddenly we were standing by, like, a biggish pond with palm trees and sand around it. Sonja had her back to us, bent over and feeding some carp. Later she said she was just tickling their heads. She turned around, real lady-like gracious for some reason, and said *Hi, you made it!* Boy, was I relieved. I thought I was gonna be stuck somewheres with those two guys, not knowing what to do.

It turned out that we were at the edge of some army R and R place, for dead soldiers of course, but set up to really make them feel like they had a week off in Thailand or somewhere. Sonja took us to the check-in desk, a kind of cross between a small hotel and an old office building. There was guys they knew there and officers and god knows what all. Tell ya the truth, I was glad to get outta there; I'd had enough for one day. When we shifted back to our level, or at least mine, I'm never exactly sure what Sonja's is, Sonja asked if I'd like more experience of that kind and I asked if I could take a rain check. She said *Sure.*

I like that about her – no pressure, no guilt tripping. She gives you the goods and you can take it or leave it, it's all the same to her. At least that's how she acts. Maybe at home with Brad she's like, *That little bitch I could slap her she's so lazy,* but with me it's like, *Hey no problem catch you later.* I dunno, maybe she's just buttering me up for something, but it sure doesn't seem like it.

12. My Useless Brothers

Goddamn them anyway. They always were assholes. Even at, like, nine or ten they were devious, sly, double-crossing pricks. There's little Melanie, all of five and full of innocence. Needless to say I got screwed every time. By the time I was in grade one, I had learned to totally ignore them and had my own group of girly girls to go with. But that's history and you don't care about that. Kid stuff really – sibling shit. Every family's the same I guess. I wouldn't know, but I guess.

A while back, not that long, it's so hard to put that kind of tag on things here, but after all the other stuff I've told you so far, I feel this pull to my mother one day. Doesn't feel any different to any other time like that, so I figure she's had a couple and is weeping in the bedroom. When I get down there, don't know why it feels like down but it does; she's pacing about between the kitchen and the dining room, chewing on her lower lip and looking not too happy. I watch and wonder. Then I sense she's worried about my brothers. One's away at college, pretending to study, and the other's working somewhere, can't remember where. I try to tune into her thoughts, but they're like chaos, everything all messed up together; stuff about Darren going to jail was mixed in with lots of other crazy stuff that I couldn't make sense of, so I just watched as she fretted about, picking things up and putting them down again, staring out the window onto the driveway. Darren's the one working. Todd's away at college. Finally the phone rang. It was my dad. Sounded like he was at a police station or something. I figured it must be dope. Darren had dealt a bit on the side for years. Maybe he got a bit cocky and took on a load he couldn't pay for. Maybe he stole some.

I can hear my mom wants to go down there and see him and I can tell my dad's trying to talk her out of it.

What do you mean bail's gonna take a while to arrange? she says, all worked up. Then something about lawyers. I can tell she's being told to calm down and be patient, and I can also tell that's like the last thing she feels like doing. Anyway, she doesn't drive so unless she's brave enough to taxi it downtown or wherever, she'll sit tight and sweat it.

I take another minute and hightail it back to my level, which, as you know, is easy. In a flash I'm back on campus and sitting down to a latte with a couple of friends. They ask why I'm antsy looking. One of them says, *No wait, I know, you've been down to see your family, right?* I nod and pull a face. When I spill what I think is the beans, Nina says, *That's nothing, my sister stabbed her boyfriend for getting another chick pregnant and nearly whacked his dad when he tried to pull them apart.* Luke nods as if to say 'I hear you'. I know from previous conversations he's been trying, with a guide's help, to stop his brother from suicide. Sounds so white trashy, I know, yet we're all from like, normal families. We'll talk about normal another time.

General consensus is I shouldn't get too breezed up about it, like what can I do anyway? I'm a ghost and who cares about us down there, we're just the past; we don't count anymore. Not that we counted for much to begin with, I wanted to add but didn't. But she had a point; we are dead, even if we don't feel like it, and we don't count to anyone back there. They make their decisions without consultation that's for sure. I guess, to be fair, we'd be the same if we were still there and them here. There's no, like, continuity. I mentioned that to Sonja once and she nodded like she agreed but said it didn't have to be that way, and maybe one day it wouldn't. When I pushed her on that she said that various people were working on some kind of earth-to-deadworld telephone and that when they got it working right life as we know it, or used to know it, would be, like, completely different. Imagine little kids being able to talk with their dead grandparents in heaven, wouldn't that totally alter their conception of life? I thought, yeah, it would.

Well, despite all those wise words I felt like getting involved. Didn't know how though. Mom never remembered anything I said when she woke up anyway. Maybe Sonja could figure a way. But what would I say anyway? *Chill out Mom, it's not as bad as it looks*? That would really work. Then I say, *Hey, I got an idea,* and the two of them look impressed. It's Andrea of course, I could maybe catch her when she's meditating, it's worked before, so why not again? They both say, *Go for it Mel,* and before you can say *chug that latte babe,* I'm off, and appearing in Andrea's apartment. Damn, it's easy traveling when you get the hang of knowing where you're going.

The place was empty when I got there, and I sat on the couch, admiring the view of the clouds passing by. Andrea suddenly walks out of the bathroom, looking all pink and clean, sits crossed legged on the carpet in front of me, and goes into her thing. After about ten minutes, her eyes closed and her body still as anything, I see the other Andrea coming out of her head like some genie out a bottle. She hangs there, floating in front of me, and slowly breaks into a smile.

I guessed you were here, she says, *what's up?*

I tell her there's some disaster with brother Darren.

Yeah that's right, she says, *he's in jail for taking some underage girl to a motel. Got her from an internet chat room, she's like thirteen, but he says she said she was eighteen. Your dad just phoned me. Could get ugly.* She was as calm as if she was talking about what to have for supper. I asked her what I should do. She said, *Nothing.* I must've scowled 'cause right away she said, *Well talk to them when they're asleep tonight, see if you can help. How's your life, what neat stuff are you getting up to?* I told her a bit about the Iraq thing and the Kurt thing. She seemed impressed and talked me up into seeing myself as some kind of superstar angel girl. Felt good for a couple of minutes and after that Andrea said she could feel the pull back into her body. With a quick smile she was gone, and I watched as she came to life and stretched. Neat how she does that. I wish more people could; Make a lot of things easier for us dead folk I'll tell ya.

So then I start thinking about Dad, and with the way things are here, in no time at all I'm standing next to him as he talks into his cell, rustling up a lawyer. I think I've met the guy once years ago – came to dinner when I was about fourteen, I think; told me I was cute at a time when I really needed the boost. You never forget things like that – well, almost never. Dad folds his cell, says something to a cop behind a counter and walks out. I bet he's going to get a coffee, or maybe something stiffer. Instead of following him out, as I could easily do, I think for a second about Darren, and there I am looking at him – the little shit. The big shit actually – five eleven at least. He's sitting with his head in his hands in a not-too-bad looking cell. I could feel sorry for him, but why? What would be the point? Let's not get into that – too ugly and boring.

I start wondering who exactly I do feel sorry for: Mom? Dad? Gran? The family reputation? and can't decide. Maybe it's just the thrill of seeing the scheming bastard caught in the web of his deceptions. He's been lying to Mom and Dad for decades; lying and cheating is his life; gets such a charge from getting away with it he can't stop – a better high than pot I'll bet. Sure I fought with the parents, all girls do, but I was always straight up rebellious, I never deceived. If they bugged me about something I'd give it to 'em straight. I may have had all my get-ups and personalities but each one of them was a straight shooter in her own way.

Curious more than anything I move close and try to feel Darren's thoughts. Oh, I get it; he's freaked that they might discover his stash inside his computer. And since he pulled the chick through the internet that'll be the first thing they'll take. Oh dear, Mr. hot shot drug dealer goes down. Then he's thinking about his girlfriend, or maybe girlfriends, I can see two or three faces flip through his aura. Yeah, that's right; I can sorta see images pass through his aura, like little photos drifting. It's pretty cool if you're in the mood. What will they say when they hear? Will they be pissed or will they think him a fuck-you hero of rebellion? Or will they even care? Maybe he can get them to testify to his terminal cool. If he got a jury of young people he'd get off. They'd see the chick was lying and looked pretty good with a push up bra and heels. How was he to know? He just wanted to fuck a stranger. What was wrong with that? Everybody did. Sure you wound up with some chick from your class and neighborhood, mostly 'cause you kinda fit, but strangers along the way were fun – an adventure, like going to Hawaii, but, like, affordable.

That was some of his thoughts. There were more, but all just about like that; a couple about my parents, mostly to do with putting on the best performance. Nothing about how messed up they might be about it. Prick! As if they didn't have enough to cope with. I thought about my dad again and was in a restaurant, nearby I guess, as he sipped on a latte and looked at a whisky as he yacked on his cell, with, let me sync in here, yeah, Andrea – figures! She tells him she's had a contact with me. I know because he repeats the word 'contact' back to her like he doesn't understand. Then he says, *Oh yes, right,* like he's trying to be polite. Maybe he doesn't believe her. I think he wants to believe but just can't quite do it. What's holding him back? He doesn't know and neither do I. Well, doubts, right, everyone has them, me too when I was alive, what else can it be. He likes Andrea, trusts her too, so it's not like she's some flaky bitch he just wants to hump. Maybe he even loves her. Most marriages go that way now, the ones that aren't fucked up from the honeymoon on. Gees most girls I know, back there anyway, haven't really got the stats for here yet – couldn't keep a guy for the weekend never mind the week or the month, me too most of the time, so I never did figure where we got off dissing our parents. They at least survived a few years.

Anyway, dad's off the phone and he's trying not to think about me, he's done enough of that by now I'll bet, but more practical stuff like lawyers and bail money. He calls some guy I don't know and asks for a loan. Must be someone he's really tight with, 'cause he doesn't, like, grovel, or anything. Maybe the guy owes him a favor. Probably does. Dad always seemed to have guys coming around and being, like, really respectful. Not like in a Sopranos Mafia kinda way, when you know it's bullshit and they'd just as soon trash the place as sip a crisp chardonnay, nor in a envious-relatives kinda way either, but more like they really did admire and respect the guy, although I couldn't tell you why. Some of them were other lawyers; *not a tribe known for their honorable ways,* he always said, grinning at me like I was sharing in a secret. Maybe they were just guys he played golf with, what do I know? I do know he loved his golf, over and above all that jazzin' the client shit that he had to do, you know charity tourneys and all that.

I wonder about Mom and I'm right there looking at her as she does something in a drawer. Mom's good at stuff like that, making work out of nothing or not very much. I'd call her on shifting dust and she'd smirk and say, *You'll be exactly the same one day, young lady, just you watch.* I bet a million American mothers said that sometime in the last year. Years! What a weird concept, to me, now, of course. Used to kind of get it, now it's like a foreign language. What can I tell you, we don't do years here; we do life without measurements. How's that? Sonja tells me that no matter how you try, you just can't explain that no-time thing to the folks down there. This thought fills me with a sudden despair. What am I doing here? I can't talk to these people. Well I can, but none of them listen, or remember. What's the use? Watching Mom mess with stuff in drawers just makes me mad, so off I go to Happydeadland, for a swim, as it turns out, in a lake that is pure and clean and sparkling. Water, that's another amazing thing here. Another time I guess. Right now I don't wanna spoil the fun by explaining it. I hope you don't mind. Notice how polite I'm getting? Back on earth I wouldn't have given a shit what you thought or felt. Dying must be good for something, I guess. Just kidding.

13. The Afterlife Gloomies

I had a couple of days – well you know – of the afterlife gloomies after all that. It just seemed to bring up all kinds of crap I thought I'd dealt with. But I'd only let it slip to the floor, where it snoozed until it was time to get up and dance around me, yapping. Crap's like that: it yaps and stinks and spills everywhere. I roamed around, walking, socializing, reading. People knew the story. Lotta kids here are in the same boat. Think I said that before somewhere, but it's true. People looked at me and kinda nodded without nodding, you know? One chick I'd seen about but hadn't talked too much, sat down beside me and said, *Family shit, huh?* Then I nodded.

She was in the mood to be a sympathetic listener and I was in the mood to be a selfish whiner, so we hit it off for a while. I could see it ending when she started on about giving it all to Jesus and to stop thinking that I could actually do anything. *Well, maybe you're right, but I'll have to think about it,* I said diplomatically as I rose to resume what had originally been a long walk. That kind of talk usually annoyed me, but I hadn't the steam to shout, like I would've in school when one of the righteous would try to read me the rule book. There used to be a few of them roaming the halls looking for converts – virgins with attitude, and me the slut that could be on the road to redemption with just a little guidance. Britney was my own little angel and would plant her plastic smile on me any chance she got. I felt groped by her gooey attentions and told her as much. She walked off in a huff and I never saw her again. Heard stories over the Christmas break; she'd transferred to a Christian high school; she'd gone off to have a baby or an abortion; she'd been raped at a party – the gossip whirled. Her little clique closed ranks in the lunchroom and kept to themselves between classes. A dope bust was the new thing. I sometimes, but not often, wonder what really happened to her.

Leaving my new best friend behind with only the tiniest of hints that her rap would be in any way useful to me, I wandered out into the country surrounding our town. It's not a town like you know them on earth, but it's closer to a town than anything I can think of. I'd heard there was a horse farm nearby and I thought sleek, beautiful horses was just what I needed. A kind of equestrian place I imagined. And the land hereabouts is like what I'd seen of Virginia horse farm country so it all kinda fit.

I found a path and followed it. I knew it was hopeless thinking that I might forget all this family shit, so I let my mind settle on it. Brooding I'd always been good at, especially the melancholy type. Last few years on earth it had been more a way of life than a mood swing. To be honest I was good at it. I could get myself into a mournful rut and stay there for days. Mom would call me Misery Mel and I'd stick my tongue out at her. But then it was easy: I knew where I stood. Family, boyfriends, school – I could figure my place in them all. Even if I didn't like that place, and I usually didn't, I could still see where it was. I could say, *Life sucks* or *School sucks big time*, and not only mean it but understand it. Now, in Happydeadland I was lost. You're probably saying, that's crazy, she's got a great life, every wish at her fingertips, no school-job-society crap, what's the problem? Well, far as I can figure, out here in the fields of heaven, it's the same family guilt trip as before. Here I am, all gone and dead and more or less thrilled with the whole thing, except for Eric really, and there they are, up to their eyes in grief and problems. What right do I have to be so free and easy?

I know what it's like. You know when you're having a blast with your buds, at a party or the movies or somewhere, getting your hair done, shopping or getting high or whatever, and you think, *Man this is the best*! And then your mom with menopause, and how she's cranky all the time, or Dad seeming to be on the edge of being let go, as he was once before (or maybe after) the merger, or those kids in Africa being used as sex slaves and soldiers, or those little Mexican kids dying by the dozen in sweat shops, and suddenly you're face to face with the big guilt trip and feel *How do I rate? What's special about me?*

I remember that I once confronted Britney on that, just to see, you know. I figured that being part of the *not perfect just saved* crowd she'd have her little mantra that would make her feel okay about being healthy and well fed while most of the planet starved and got fucked over by whoever held the whip and had the whim. She looked all serious and said something about putting it all in God's hands and all those suffering would be redeemed in heaven. I said *Muslims and Hindus too?* She made a face and said she wasn't sure about that. Maybe they'd be converted when they got there and saw how Jesus was right all along. Yes, she was sure they'd have a chance. Jesus was like infinitely merciful. I didn't buy it, but I said I'd think about it. Liar; I never thought about it really, I mean her point. She was just babbling, repeating something someone in church had told her. Most of the planet gets royally screwed every minute of every day, while the handful of rich folks, like you and me, get to worry about our hair and our cars and our credit cards.

Speaking of Muslims, there's that girl down the hall from me, Maryam or something. She reads the Koran a lot, now that she's in heaven and surrounded by Christians or kids that were born that way and now don't give a shit. She's trying to figure it out too. She says her family was secular even before they left Iran and came to L.A., but now she's in heaven or someplace like it, she figures she better, like, get a grip on what she thinks. I said to forget it and just have fun like the rest of us, but she shook her head like, *I dunno.* I knew for a fact there were a bunch of Iranian guys just desperate to get laid 'cause they'd died virgins, and let it slip as she looked like one herself, with her prim manners and legs, like, roped together. I knew 'cause I met them in the dance clubs we got here and got propositioned by every one of them. I wonder what Britney would say to see her here now. Probably figure she's on some waiting list to get saved. I mean, how else could a not-really-religious Muslim be here? She has her own Sonja that comes to visit her and she looks like she might have been a Muslim lady at one time. Those dark, smoldering eyes and that beautifully carved profile; she looks a bit like one of those Iranian real estate ladies I seen in one of Mom's magazine articles, one of whom said – and I'll never forget this for some reason – that she'd sooner die than go back to Iran under the mullahs.

This is all a ways from my melancholy brooding, as I traipse through these fields of long wavy grass, wondering if the horse place is maybe just beyond that next line of trees, which is maybe a good thing – I don't know. I flop down beside a big old tree and suck on a stem of grass, just like I did on earth. For all the stuff that's different here there's still a lot the same. The daydreaming I do is not so different from the daydreaming I used to do. Okay, so maybe there's less mystery to worry about, but there's still, like, a lot of stuff that you'd like to piece together but can't. Maybe this confusion is the essence of being a teenager, even though I'd be well into my twenties if I was still there. Unlike that old song that Eric downloaded from somewhere that he loves to quote, confusion will *not* be my epitaph. Least I don't see how it can be now that I'm here.

I did wander out of those woods and came across the wonderful horses – all different kinds, all beautiful. They were mostly wandering around like me. None of them seemed melancholy though. Grazing, trotting, cantering, drinking from a pond, whatever they were doing they seemed perfectly at ease. Horses in heaven I guess. I sat against a tree and just watched. Eventually a couple of riders came by – young women, not much older than me. I waved, they waved back. It was so natural, so careless, so just like life, as if we'd never died, any of us. If only I could get people to understand that. If only I could understand it myself. But at least the brooding had just about bled itself dry. I strolled back to town not quite happy but definitely less stressed. I knew I should be thinking about Eric instead of myself, so I made up my mind to do something special for him next time he was asleep, which would not be long, and which probably you've been wondering about.

Sonja advised me ages ago that if I got to communicating with people back on earth the time issue would be something they'd want explained. She gave me about ten ways to put it and right now I can't recall any of them. This countryside is just too beautiful and I can't concentrate on that technical stuff.

So, if there's no night here (and there isn't, least not where I stay) and we don't sleep much, although we can if we want and a lot do when they first arrive, I did for sure; how do we know when it's night on earth? For me it's like telepathy. I mean, we get telepathic stuff from family and friends a lot, but after you've rushed down there to respond and find them walking about or sitting having coffee or weeping over old photographs and they don't pay the slightest attention to your, *Hey it's me, I'm here!* stuff, you learn to discern the *subtleties in the transmission*. You guessed it, that's Sonja's phrase not mine. I could have faked it I guess, but you wouldn't have bought it, would you? So when Eric's getting out of his body and thinking of me I just know. It's different than when he's having a hard time during the day in his wheelchair and wishes he were with me or something. It's like a whistle of a different pitch. Or like the different ways someone can pinch you. Does that help? It's the best I can do right now. Some people say they see little flashes in front of their eyes, but I don't – at least not yet. People tell me it could happen any time. I know, just one more crazy thing about life here.

I returned to my rooms and waited, relaxing. The view from my bedroom window was beautiful and sometimes I felt like I could relax there forever: tennis courts then woods and then hills stretching away. I could human watch or nature watch. Sonja had said a lot of what I saw was created by souls who have been here long long before me, including the idea of clouds. Like the clouds aren't clouds but someone's idea of clouds. That's what she claims. Hard to believe as they're the loveliest big puffy clouds you ever did see. She told me not to get my knickers in a twist over it and I didn't. What you do is up to you. I'm just passing along what I've been told.

Finally I got the feeling from Eric and willed myself to his bedroom. Sure enough, there he was, sitting at his desk reading – just like old Eric. Well, it *was* old Eric, he was just obe. We hugged and kissed. He was still a bit shy, even though he'd known me since grade three. I was determined to get him out and away from his bedroom, so I listened patiently as he told me about his day. Obviously things, even the simplest, are way more complicated when you're in a wheelchair. Even me, Miss Flying Deadgirl, knew that. After some talk and some intimacy that I don't care to go into right now, I told Eric I wanted to take him flying. I was expecting some resistance, but he went right for it. *Okay I'm game,* were his exact words. I did the old close-your-eyes-and-hold-my-hand stuff and in a second we were outside the house floating up over the rooftops. He was amazed of course. We moved slowly up to the clouds and then into them and then out the top. I asked if he wanted to fly about instead of just float. He opened his eyes wide and said, *Yeah!*

That was all I needed to hear. Off we went, zipping this way and that, down through clouds and then up and around them again. I'd been getting slowly better at my gliding seagull impression – you know how they are – so I showed him how to do that on his own. He was a quick learner and was soon dive bombing me as I wheeled about. Man, what total fun!

He didn't actually have to go back, but for some weird reason he felt he ought to – just too exciting I guess. His bedroom seemed lovely and nest-like after our adventures. After some quiet time, he said he felt the urge, kissing me deeply and disappeared back into his body. I slipped onto the bed beside him, but as he looked like he was never gonna wake up, left him and returned to my own Happydeadland, feeling kinda good about myself too, which was likely what I needed then. After a rest and a swim, I sat in on another History of American Folk music lecture. Not only that, I signed up for some dulcimer lessons – always loved the sound of that. Heard it somewhere years before but didn't even know what one looked like.

14. Another Time on the Island

This time I went by myself – getting my confidence up I guess. Plus I wanted to see how Lisa was doing; okay as it turned out. Well, that's what I heard anyway. She'd made some friends and gone on a picnic. So I sat around the recreation room of the mansion place and played cards for a while with three girls I'd just met: Dani, Franka, and Sue – all teen hookers from different towns: West coast, Alaska via the Midwest, Florida somewhere. Maybe I got that wrong, but who cares really? They were from all over but that didn't stop them from having lousy childhoods, crappy families, junky mothers, you name it. Is it any wonder chicks get so fucked up? Dani had overdosed on something, choked on her vomit maybe, she wasn't sure. Franka called it quits after three abortions and jumped off some bridge and Sue couldn't quite get her head around being a Pentecostal gay. That was her exact words, I swear. Don't know about you but I just freaked. A Pentecostal dyke? Too funny. Couldn't take the denial she said straight-faced. She was a bit older than the other two, and, like, way hipper. I called her on it and she leant over and sucked my face for a minute. No doubt about it, girl had style. I figured her for an adventurous bi more than anything, but doing the dyke thing to impress the two teenies.

Not long after that they called it quits to go do their nails. Never got into nails much myself, except for the black and red phase, which kinda had me in its grip there for a while. But I'm dead now and way past all that silly stuff. So Suze and I decide to go for a walk. There's plenty of woodsy stuff around the buildings and we just follow the first path we see. Suze, natch, has a story and is itching to tell it. She acts out a lot, you know gestures, and acting out all the parts in any scene she's telling you. Kept reminding me of Winona Ryder in *Girl, Interrupted,* and I told her. She was, like, so pleased, that's one of her all time faves. That and *Reality Bites.*

She's had a rough life, Suze has. Wow, I'm thinking, glad that wasn't me. Compared to her I'm little Miss Spoiltrichgirl. White trash in Miami might be better than white trash in Muncie, Indiana or Lincoln, Nebraska, or Portland, Oregon, but it's still white trash. You still got daytime soaps and crack under the floorboards and there's always someone you know just getting out of jail. Her own mother tried to turn her out for dope money. She stole the secret stash, sold it, and took the Greyhound to Jacksonville and then hitched to Tucson. *God musta smiled,* she said, 'cause her second ride was a totally out-there-old hippy couple who took pity on her and put her up at their home, kind of out in the boonies, but you know – safe. Turns out they were churchy Christians, but they didn't lay it on too thick. First breakfast they tell her they've prayed for guidance and the guidance said, *Don't send her back even though she's sixteen. Adopt her as your own.* So they set her up as the niece from Alaska whose mother had died and the locals seemed to like it, or didn't care at all. The school records were a problem, but the new principal guy was one of the congregation and was in on the plan, so he faked it somehow: cool guy, like a Christian Sean Penn. Nice school too, but kids ask questions and she wasn't always believed. Alaska with that tan? Please. So she freaked and ran off. Well, hitched – all the way to Phoenix, which is big enough to hide in. She found some street kids squatting somewhere and joined them. Holyee, it was back to cuss words, drugs and casual sex. She wasn't used to that now, was she? I laughed, sure I laughed. You should have seen her – panhandling, stealing, jail. Bummer! Some juvenile detention center. Looks like they're gonna ship her back to Miami. She runs off one night, finds a bridge jumps off it. *Fuck that,* she says, *I'd sooner die.* Then she's dead, floating around, kinda free and happy. I walked, she floated right away. Doesn't know why. Anyway it's way more fun than going back to Miami. She'd always figured there'd be some kinda something after, she just didn't know what. Met another dead kid, then another, kinda floated around together for a while, went to California, floated slowly over the ground, not knowing they could go fast. Fun though, looking down at all the grass and trees and hills and rivers and stuff. Got to Big Sur or someplace like it. Lived on the beach – beach ghosts. That was a blast: swimming, flying, cookouts, sunbathing – two guys and her. Then a couple more girls, down from Frisco – dead like them: street kids gunned down in a deal gone bad – least that's what they said. Jealousy shit coming on. Was better with just the two guys, she was the star – star fuck too. Then this surfer dude comes by. Looks like he's dead, but maybe not. Acts so cool and like, knowledgeable. Asks them if she wants to check out heaven. Everyone thinks that it sounds totally uncool. Heaven? That's for, like, good people, right? People with jobs and haircuts and cars. But Suze likes the guy and says, *Yeah, I'll check it out*. He brings her here, simple as that. That was like three days ago. Or whatever, she's not sure. *What's a day here?* she asks me.

Good question Suze. Lemme tell ya a couple of stories.

So I tell her some of the stuff you've heard about already and more I guess. That's 'cause I get mixed up with what I've told you and what I haven't. And I am not about to take notes. School's out for me, but I guess if I take more courses, even if it's stuff I want, I'll be back at it. Oh well, it was fun while it lasted. We sat down on some logs and I continued my story. Of course it all sounds like a rich girl's fantasy life to Suze, who doesn't sound like she had more than three nutritionally balanced meals in her life. Sound like my mother, right?

There's a neat kind of intimacy when you share stories like we did that day. It's something I've always loved, and something you don't get very often, even here. I was right in the middle of some story when these other girls came by and asked if they could sit with us. They seemed kinda gloomy and I thought Suze was gonna blow them away with some outrage. All of them looked about fourteen. Only one of them spoke really, girl called Alice, and she didn't say much – mostly stuff about being murdered by the neighborhood psycho and wandering about her home town trying to talk to her girlfriends and watching her family stumble about grieving. I was about to chip in with a comment about being lucky as most neighborhoods have at least three psychos, but the thing about the family grieving struck home too quick and I shut up. The other two looked like they wanted to be asked how they died so I asked, figuring it'd be some kind of x-rated horrorshow. It was – they both were: junkie sex slavery with a side of hepatitis followed by quick and dirty disposal. Been moved from city to city in vans, so no one would really catch on. Not that the johns cared anyway – just wanted their rocks off and out the door. I guessed they were all relieved to be dead, but most everyone is here, it's like the norm, you take it for granted, like you take being pissed at your parents for standard down there.

Alice had a bit more to say, but it was all fourteen year old stuff; hadn't ever gotten to kiss her grade seven boyfriend – not really, not like a real kiss. I thought about myself in that grade, but kept quiet. I did tell her that she could maybe try visiting him while he was asleep, but she looked at me like I was mad, so I let it go. The other two hadn't had the luxury of boyfriends, even ones they hadn't kissed. I wondered if they were kissing each other, but didn't say anything. But you hear about stuff like that. But she did say something weird that some writer was coming to visit her about her life story. She wasn't sure how she was doing it, 'cause this woman was, like, still alive. I wondered what would make this chick's story interesting, she was such a dweeb really – talk about self-obsessed. Then I remembered something Sonja had told me about sometime, that artists and writers come to Happydeadland while they're asleep, experience some stuff and then go back and make their half-or-even-quarter-remembered experiences into some kind of art without really knowing what they've done. Writers write books about people in heaven, and call them novels; artists paint pictures of this world and call it fantasy, and musicians, she says, kinda do the same, although I'm not too clear on how exactly.

After a while they all got up and left. You know, the little procession thing. Suze and I looked at each other like, *Bye, see ya!* They were so... young. Being dead doesn't make you suddenly like kids you wouldn't have been around for five seconds before. 15 and 20 just don't mix that well. Suze and I walked some more, chatting and laughing like friends from way back. I suggested a swim and she kinda freaked. Took me a moment and then I guessed it: she hadn't been here long enough to know that you could swim with your clothes on here. She didn't believe me when I told her they dried instantly when you got out and didn't even weigh you down like they would on earth. So I just waded in and started swimming, then she followed, squealing and laughing. It was cool.

As we walked back through the woods to the residence place I wondered if I should invite Suze to my place. I told her it was filled with guys and girls just about her age and would be great fun, but something seemed to be holding her back. She thanked me and said she'd think about it. Later I wondered if I'd made a mistake talking about the college town atmosphere. That was true, it really did feel like that, and not by accident either, but she'd never had much of an education so maybe she was worried about being out of her depth or something. So I said *Sure, maybe another time then,* and gave her a little hug, which seemed to, like, make her glow, and walked off to the waterside to look for one of those cute little boats.

15. My Residence

I was sitting in one of the lounges sometime later, watching one of the earth channels. Somehow or other we got some of the earth TV stuff here. Don't know how they pull it off, but then there it is – Oprah upon the wall. We got our own Happydeadworld channels too, but a lot of people really want to see that old earth programming, like their favorite bands on MTV and stuff. Soaps too, you can just imagine. Think of all the soap addicts you know, then think of them dead. See? They still need their fix. Same with other stuff I guess. I love my dancing and partying, and there's religious kids who still go to church faithfully every week, sometimes two or three times. Lots of people doing modern ballet, jazz dance and gymnastics; I mean like really into it, like they'd been starved before. You should see the two golf courses, line-ups every morning. Not that we really have mornings here. I mean you rest, you take it easy, but you only really sleep for a bit after you first get here. Mostly because you figure you ought to. It's like the habit of sleepiness without the exhaustion – or something.

So I'm watching some kinda news show thing, catching up on all the crap. Half so I can talk to Eric about it and half 'cause I'm still half on earth I think. Maybe I shouldn't go down there so much. Maybe I should really practice being here, 'cause after all, I'm here to stay. It's not like a vacation, where you get your jollies and go home to the rack and thumb screws. It feels like a vacation, sure, and a lot of the newbies are convinced it is – a dream vacation with an alarm clock at the end – but it's not. This isn't a rehearsal for the real deal, it is the real deal.

[illegible]m watching away, it's CNN and it all seems so, like, who-[illegible]ring. I was never much interested before, but I'm even [illegible] Dad usta say it was all about being a good citizen, [illegible]rmed, knowing what was going on, but Mom would say she couldn't follow it all, there was way too much to keep track of, and most of it too sad or depressing. Dad would get annoyed with her and she would sing, in that funny squeaky voice of hers, that Paul Simon song, *My father was a fisherman, my mother was a fisherman's friend*, except she'd change the words to *My husband was a citizen and I was a citizen's friend*. All that war stuff, the arguing about why it was necessary and who was to blame, and that hokey intelligence. How'd that CIA guy get to keep his job anyway? Dad always said the Agency and the Bureau never could work together on anything – that you might as well ask the Russians to help out. Eric says he gets emails from a guy who claims the Mossad offered to take out all those flying Mohammeds over a weekend but that the Agency said they'd think it over. Eric's one of those Pearl Harbor guys: you know; they knew it was gonna happen but they let it so they'd have everyone on side for the oil war. Kids at school said it was the crusades all over again, and that they'd get to Jerusalem eventually. Actually, it was just one guy who said that but it sounded so cool a lot of people just grabbed it and suddenly it was like official lunchroom policy. Though they didn't say much, the Iranian kids – there's about eight of them, guys and girls – didn't seem to care one way or the other; they're all, like, westernized, and mullah-free. Like especially the girls, who ain't ever going back, no matter what. *What you want,* Arlene said when I asked, *you think I'm some kinda crazy bitch who wants to get slapped around for the rest of her life by some Arab retard who never shaves? Get a fuckin' life Mel*. An Iranian guy walked over and started to, like, disagree. She gave him about two seconds before calling him a sick fuck who jerked off to pictures of eleven year old virgins in his spare time. Another chick came over and offered to stick a couple of cold French fries up his butt for a buck. Too heavy for me, so I left them to it, I had a class to go to.

Then there's a thing about abortions and abstinence and STD's and shit: the just-say-no crowd – so goddamn saintly. Bet they'r all got underpaid illegals as maids and nannies. They can take their moral standards to the cleaners for all I care. I can live without them. Then something about coal mining in Kentucky, lung disease and shit. Like, where's the good news? Like people surfing in Hawaii or snowboarding in Colorado or some big open air concert with everyone cooked on mushrooms and groovin'? Well, wouldn't you know it, then there was something about Mardi Gras in New Orleans – costumes and parades and dancing. Cool. Never did go. Sonja tells me you can go anywhere as a ghost and I guess she's right, but it's easy to forget, and as I told you I think, there's so much to do here anyway. Just then someone flops down beside me and asks what's up. It's that Muslim girl from down the hall – finally made it out of her room. I congratulate her. She lowers her eyes and sorta smiles. She's been reading the Koran again, she says. I thought she'd never put it down since I first met her, but I didn't say that. It looked funny, but I could see she was no worse than lots of others looking for some answers in the holy books. Anyway, she's decided to see what life is all about here, instead of sitting in her room wondering.

I start to worry that she's maybe decided to nominate me as her guide, but no, she says she's all set for an adventure and bounces up and away with a cute little wave. I try to recall if she's got any friends or family here but can't. Not that it seems to matter much. Those that do don't seem any happier really. Usually it's grandparents anyway, and college-age types like us don't have much use for that right now. We only just got rid of parental authority, we don't need more. I got three myself and I could do without all of them.

Ken and Julia, my dad's parents, have been in this world for a while: three or four years earth time. They died in a car crash on a foggy night and came together, least that's what they told me. I mean it's probably true; they did die in a crash and were pronounced D.O.A. at the hospital, so why not? Even if they were seventy-eight or whatever, it did seem romantic. Their kids were set for life; they'd sold their house and traveled some. You know, they hadn't missed much. Well, that's what my dad said. They'd had falling outs through the years and weren't exactly close when they died, so I wondered when they came to see me right off. Showed up at this little bed and breakfast type place Sonja brought me to after the accident with Eric. Bit kind of formal and stiff, but they were always like that, reserved I guess you'd say. Julia brought me some lovely flowers and Ken a book – just like I was sick in hospital. Actually the book was great. *How I Survived Dying* it was called. By some chick who was religious and when she passed went to some religious heaven place and then decided she didn't like it, but couldn't get away 'cause the leaders wouldn't let her go – like a cult thing but on a really big scale. Anyway it was interesting and kinda funny in the end. Why Ken gave it to me I never did figure.

Anyway, they invited me to stay at their house when I got my strength back. Actually I felt fine, but as people kept insisting I should rest I did. Hey, I can sit up in bed, read magazines and eat cookies with the best of them. So after a bit, I went to their place. They had a beautiful house and lovely garden, just like they did before. It even looked the same. Well not exactly, but close – like they'd asked for a replica. Actually, they'd remodeled from another style. Well, they put me in an upstairs bedroom for a bit – nice and quiet, with a beautiful view of a lake in the distance. I felt quite privileged and flounced about like a little princess for a while, nibbling goodies and reading novels, going for walks around the lake and boating with them in their little yacht – very relaxing and ego rebuilding. That may sound funny, but I felt like that's what happened. Dying kind of shattered me for a while. I needed space to put myself together again. Even watching Julia as she gardened – and boy did she garden – helped. I was like someone after a nervous breakdown. At least Ken thought so. Said he wasn't surprised, being cut off so suddenly from my family and way of life. They at least had each other and their life had only been interrupted for short while, and what they had now was better than anything they had before. Relatives and friends they had at a distance, which was just fine. In a way they were still enjoying their retirement. And as you can imagine, the retired life became a bit too slow for me, once I'd become me again.

Sonja'd been coming by once in a while for afternoon tea, which Julia just loved. Gracious afternoon teas were really her style, and since I left I've never had another, and I think Sonja was doing more than just being polite and keeping an eye on me. But who knows, I never asked. After tea one day Sonja and I went for a walk. She asked if I was still happy here. I told her I was getting a bit antsy for some action, so she told me about the place I live now. Sounded great and just what a babe in my predicament needed. I didn't take much convincing, I'll tell ya. And maybe that's to Sonja's credit, knowing I was ready.

My other grandfather, well that's another story – drank himself into an early grave is the family version, and as far as I can figure, that's right. Gran never spoke of him when I was a kid and later was too into politics to talk about anything else. After I'd gotten settled into my Happydeadland college town, which by the way has a different name every week as jokesters keep changing the sign, I asked Sonja about him. How would I find out where he was, I wanted to know. She checked and told me I probably didn't want to know. A dump in one of the lower astrals, she told me, a dump with plenty of bars and gambling. Like that area I showed you some chapters back, but worse I think. Anyway I never went, and don't really regret it, although maybe I will one day.

Enough video idiocy; I get up and walk away, brave girl that I am. I'll show that TV who's boss. The cafeteria seems like a good bet and I grab a spinach salad and a pop. It's hard to figure out if you're hungry here; I'm starting to wonder if it really is just a habit, as Sonja says. Anyway, it's still fun and you can pretty well get anything you want. You can suck up fast food junk from day till night if you want and many do, especially after you first get here and find out that there's no gaining weight. You should see the anorexics wolfing down cheeseburgers! Too funny!

I'm munching away and flipping through a magazine when a couple of my buds drop by. Grant's just come from an architecture lecture and Monica's been to dance class, and both of them are like totally buzzed. Grant says he didn't understand half of what he heard but the rest was a total mind blower. And to get it from a guy who worked with Frank Lloyd Wright – that was too much. Monica's been a dancer since she was five – bit of ballet, bit of jazz, bit of, I dunno, a lot of different stuff from around the world: you know, colorful native costumes and the whole bit. She says I gotta come and at least watch; the stuff they can do here, with the almost-no-gravity situation, is amazing. It's all she can do to stop herself flying. In fact, there's a class rule: no flying. All that leaping twirling ballet stuff is a breeze. Real ballet types must be bored here, she thinks, everything is way too easy. I tell her I've heard guys say the same about basketball. Grant adds golf is becoming much the same, everyone's figuring out how to direct the ball with their minds and get a hole in one, and once you've got that down it sure becomes a bore – no challenge. Together we wonder if life gets boring here after a while. It sure sounds like it could. I wonder if my dulcimer lessons will be so easy. Well, I'll find out soon, my first class is coming up.

Grant tells us about his last date. Turns out she was a Mormon virgin and desperate to get laid. I just shrugged and chuckled, but Monica wanted to know why he felt he had to tell us. Didn't that girl have some privacy rights? Grant thought she was being a shit; she'd told us about dates, what's the difference? Her dates weren't virgins – that's special. Grant told her to get a life. Monica flapped off, doing a pisspoor imitation of being insulted I thought. *What was that all about?* I asked Grant when she left. *You guys got issues I don't know about?*

Search me, was his reply.

I thought, *Hmmn, something there,* but we'll let that little doggie lie. He asked me what I was doing. I said, not much, besides my dulcimer class. He suggested we get one of the little rowboats and take it over to one of the islands in the lake. There's about three or four of them – couple are mainly for picnicing and camping, couple are bird sanctuaries.

Course you don't actually row across. This is the afterlife, you think your way across. Thought is your engine, as I think Sonja said to me back when I was a newbie. We had a fun time together, and wound up getting it on under the trees. We'd only been buds up until then and I'd never really considered him potential before. He seemed like a lot of guys here, amazed to get laid so often. I don't think he cared for me in any special way, just a natural attraction. Hey, what can I say, a babe's a babe and I'm one. Don't take no special talent, far as I can see. Although it sure is easier here than on earth with all that STD and pregnancy shit hanging over your head. It was only on the way back that I started to get to feeling guilty. Guilty about what? Eric of course. Could you cheat on someone when they were still there and you here? I dunno, but I sure wasn't gonna tell him about Grant, he was way too fragile for that. Grant asked what was up. I'd already told him about Eric's condition, so I just had to mention the name. Grant had left a girlfriend behind on earth himself, so he could understand. He wasn't visiting with her that I knew of, had said she took up with someone else a month after he passed, so I didn't pester him about it. But we did share and I was grateful. Lotta guys won't do that.

16. Nighttime On Earth

Well that's the time I'm there most often, so it seems like a good thing to be talking about. I mean, you want to know, don't you, what it's like for us, to have to snoop about your dark and quiet houses looking for the odd soul who wants to wake up and talk. First off, I don't sneak into strangers' houses like some nosy bitch, and I don't know anyone who does, although Sonja tells me many are tempted and can't resist, I only go where I know people, and that's really only Eric, my family, and Andrea's place. I did check out a few of my old girlfriends from high school when I first came over, but none of them even noticed while they were awake and slept like babies inside their bodies for the whole night. Sonja tells me there's no way to tell ahead of time if people will emerge from sleep or not. The only way to find out is to go there and watch. *Eric,* she said, *has the real strong desire to get out and does so.* I asked if he would've before the accident and she said she'd check but I haven't heard back from her on that one. I wonder how she'd find out anyway. Andrea seems like a natural somehow; maybe it's the meditation that helps. It's always been then when I've met up with her. Tonight is the first time I've, like, calmly and carefully, thought of going to her sleeping body and seeing if she comes out. Outside her building I stop and think: do I have a right to do this? Probably not, but I don't think she'll mind. We're pretty much friends now.

I kinda dither outside her bedroom, again nervous about butting in. It's just that she's about the only person on earth that I can sorta connect with. Well Eric too, of course, but with him it's me caring for him and his issues, nothing wrong with that, right, but with Andrea I can, Oh I dunno, level with her I guess. I suppose I can with Sonja too, but what I have in mind is more Andrea than Sonja. As I'm hovering there – I was gonna say standing, but I was actually hovering – guess what, Andrea comes through the bedroom door. Yeah, through, just like I told you about before. Doesn't seem to see me at first so I kinda wave my hands in front of her face, like *Hey you there! Wake up!* And whammo, she's like awake suddenly. (Way later Sonja tells me that quite a few physicals, as she calls them sometimes, float out of their bodies and drift about only half aware for hours and then drift right back, slotting in just before dawn, but I didn't know that then). She smiles and hugs me right away, which does me a lot of good, 'cause I feel better about myself right away. Just like people in their bodies we move to the couch and lay back to chat; habit really, as ghosts like us don't feel that body-needing-to-relax stuff – not really. Earth habits I guess, they're like second nature. You do 'em without thinking. It's amazing really, just how earthlike our conversation is. She asks how my new life is going, what I've been up to recently, that kinda stuff, and basically I tell her. It's just like I've been away at college, which in a way, I have. I ask her about Dad, kinda tip-toeing around the affair issue, and sure enough that brings up the brother-in-jail issue, although he's got bailed out now apparently.

Darren's like sedated; he's so screwed up she says. Mom gave him some of her calm-yourself-down-lady pills and the two of them flaked out on either ends of the couch. Andrea knows this 'cause Dad phoned a couple hours back and told her. Brother Todd has gone to stay with his buddy Mike across town. I got a couple of things to say about Mike, but I'll keep them to myself for now. Strange though, it seems like years since he and Todd were close. Instead I tell Andrea about Mom naming Darren 'Darwin' at birth and Darren hating it from the get-go and always wanting to be called Darren or Dart. She finds those stories so funny I feel, like, brave, and tell her about Mike trying to rape me in my bedroom when I was like, thirteen. To this day I'm not really sure, but it was weird the way my door was suddenly, like, closed and hard to open. Where Todd disappeared to, I dunno, but I can guess. Mike wasn't that big a guy and I was feisty and full of beans, so in seconds we're like wrestling on the floor and he's trying to get my pants off. Can't remember where I got the idea at that age, but I knew to grab his balls and squeeze. For about two seconds he thought he was on to a good thing but then it was curtains for his daddy years unless he could, like, suffocate me or something. Then he began to like beg and groan and go red. I kept it up. He punched me, hard – real hard. Somehow I got him off me, jumped up, nose bleeding, crying, and tried to open the door. It was stuck somehow – glued or something. He started to get up. I turned and kicked him in the belly. He stayed down. The prick, I thought, he was never like this before, what's his problem? I finally got the door open and rushed to the bathroom to wash my face. A lot of cold water stopped the bleeding somehow, but my face looked like I'd been attacked by a cat. I vowed to make him pay. He wasn't in my bedroom anymore and I didn't think to look in Todd's.

Mom I found out in the garden shed, repotting plants – big gardener my mom. Todd was there too, talking to her about more lunch money or something. He did a pretty good job of looking shocked, but I knew he was in on it, 'cause he had that same look in his eyes as when I accused him of peeing into my doll's house kitchen when I was, like, six.

Considering I'd been fighting non-stop with Mom since the bleeding began, my chick blood that is, not the nose stuff, she was pretty good about it. Well I guess it was obvious shit had happened. Right away she said to Todd, *Where's Mike?*

Gone to the bathroom, Todd said. Todd had this way of looking like an innocent angel that Mom fell for every time, right up until he was caught shoplifting at the mall. Boy did it piss me off. The mall thing was about a year in the future then, so it was still choir boy Todd then. After the shoplifting charge he started murmuring about the minister, the one now fortunately in Mongolia doing missionary work, fondling him, but I knew it was bullshit, 'cause it was going around the schoolyard about some other priest somewheres who'd just gotten busted or something. Course I was skipping church and Mom didn't like that, but shit, Dad hadn't gone for year – something to do with Vietnam probably; that was his reason for everything.

So Mom charges off to find Mike locked in the upstairs bathroom refusing to come out. Or at least that's what she tells me when I see her in the kitchen as I'm about to drink some water. I tip the glass, gulp and tell her to leave it to me. She looks stunned for just long enough for me to get out of the room and up the stairs. I kicked the bathroom door and shouted *Mike! You get out here and face the music! Now!* Like I said, I was a feisty one, but where I got the nerve for that I don't know. I kicked the door again.

I'm not coming out till your mom's there. Course she arrives in time to hear that and gives me this look.

Mike, I'm here you can come out. She pushes me away from the door and sorta glares at me. The door opens a crack and Mike's weasel face peeps out. Mom tells him it's okay, the coast is clear. I stifled a chuckle. It was then I knew she was on my side. So when she told me to go to my room I did. Mike was lead downstairs and questioned with Todd. Mom then came up to me. It was one of those mother-daughter things where it was the real Mom and the real me. No bullshit, no wait-till-I-tell-your-father. Mike kinda melted into the background after that.

So I tell all this to Andrea and she tells me about a date rape thing that happened to her a few years ago. Nothing too frantic, just one of those second bottle of wine misunderstandings that got outta hand. She wasn't battered and bruised as much as baffled and feeling dumb. The guy wasn't much happier. He'd figured she wanted a bit of rough stuff and was obliging her and he looked so sincere when he said it she believed him. She guessed she should've fought back more but lost heart. I asked if she felt sorry for him – I have on occasion. Like some guys seem to need it so bad you do it just make them feel better.

Anyway we went on like this for ages, hours maybe – chick talk. I even ask her about Dad, like he was someone else's dad and not mine. She looks relieved for a moment, like she was maybe expecting me to freak out somehow. Maybe it's because I'm dead and not gonna be affected like I might be on earth, you know, child of the broken family thing, but I can't seem to do the shocked daughter routine at all. Andrea's happy, though maybe not totally thrilled with the way the relationship's going. She figures Dad's gonna stay with Mom after all, that she's just the affair babe, the mid-life trophy chick. Looking at her I think I can see her point. She's got the figure, the face and the poise. And I tell her as much. I don't mention the crow's feet or the impending double chin, but hey she's thirty-nine not twenty-four. Dad's, like, fifty-five and chubby, despite the endless squash, so she's likely a babe to him. Mom's kinda motherly if you know what I mean – more Barbara Bush than Hilary Clinton. Okay, I admit it, Gran said it first, when her back was turned. I said she looked a bit like Barbara Bush herself. She fired me one of her looks and said, *Mel, I'm seventy-nine; your mom's forty-eight. Get a life.*

Gran's funny like that. You'd swear she was hangin' with teenagers sometimes. Well I guess she is, some of those peace activist anti-globalization types are. She thrills them with talk about the Chicago Eight. Or was it seven? I never could get that straight. Swears she had a fling with Abbie Hoffman too. Don't think I believe that, but Dad said you never know. He was away from home at the time and his sister off at college, or so he says. Hey, Abbie Hoffman's dead like me, maybe I could find him and ask him. But maybe he wouldn't remember. Can't you just see it; *Hey Abbie, how's it goin'? And I was just wondering, did you, like, once have a fling with my gran*? Too funny.

Andrea then tells me about a weird experience when she was thirteen. With her own brother, but not quite so violent. No real damage she figures, just a bit of teen kinkiness. They both knew it wasn't right somehow and kind of kept their distance after that one time, although they were pretty good friends. He got into music production after college and now runs a jazz club in Copenhagen. *Wow,* says I, not quite remembering where that is – Europe sure, but where? She asks me if I'm still seeing Eric. I tell her sure, almost every night when he's out of his body. Does he feel suicidal sometimes, she wants to know. Not much as far as I can tell. Depressed sometimes, yes. Suicidal? I don't think so. He's working on trying to bring his OBE stuff into his life and, like, tell people – not much success so far. Mostly they indulge him, like, *Oh really that's nice for you,* but behind his back he's sure they're like just feeling sorry for him, you know, cripple-boy-dreams-of-flight type stuff.

Anyway, I talk to Andrea so long that by the time I get to Eric's place he's back in his body, all wrapped up in sleep. Who knows, maybe he wasn't out at all, how would I know really? That's what I tell myself anyway. On impulse, I float around my old neighborhood as the dawn comes on – a sentimental journey on all my old paths here and here. Cutting through the park to get to school, that little bit of woody stuff behind the mall where we used to smoke, Eric's great backyard that just kind of melted into the forest area of the park, where we used to hang out on sunny days, all secluded and safe. I'm sitting there, in this lovely early morning light that I never used to see when I was alive, when I feel like, I dunno, God is with me or something – one of those special moments when everything seems to stop breathing, or shares the same breath, or something.

Sonja says God is always with you, even if you don't know it. I remember church guys saying the same thing on Earth. If you don't know it what good does it do? That's what I say. Sonja says I just have to hold the thought in my mind, never did ask the ministers, too cool for that. Anyway it's just a feeling, you don't see anything. Even ghosts like me don't see anything. Most of the time you don't want to anyway. Really, it's enough being dead and all. And what would you say anyway? What's it all about? Why all the crap, the cancer and suffering and war? Why can't U2 play smaller venues? I don't know what's scarier, having him show up for question time, or the idea that he might actually have answers: answers that make perfect sense and you wonder why no one ever said them before. Personally, I don't think he talks at all. Why would he-she bother? What's there to say? It's all happening, everything, the sun rising, the wind blowing, newspapers being read, music danced to, books being written and stuff, cells multiplying and dying; why pick one detail of the endless activity and make it stand out from the rest? What makes that one detail more important? That's what I'd like to know. Brought that up at dinner once back on earth. Got everyone going – well the adults. Todd said, *Who gives a shit*. But Dad told him time out, that it was an interesting point. But he had to admit he didn't really have a good answer. Some things seemed more important at certain times, and others at others. Mom piped up with something about agendas. Darren suddenly cut a huge fart. Todd giggled; the rest of us scowled. Dad asked him if he'd rather talk about baseball. Darren said, *Sure*. Dad said, *Okay, after dinner then*.

But it blew the mood. I said, *Looks like Darren's agenda wins out*. Dad said not so, but he'd forgotten to turn his cell off and some client guy called and Mom and I went to talking about Nicole's new pond. Nicole's our neighbor. Anyway, I think I spent some time on this God stuff before, didn't I? But it just kinda came up again, here in this sunny quiet backyard in the morning, with just a few birds and me – the genial ghost. Love that word, genial, it's so... genial.

So I'm grooving away, just so calm and cool I can't believe it, like suddenly nothing really matters, not life, not death, not guys, not family; no fear, no anxiety, no excitement, and no God stuff either. Just this huge cloud of calmness and I'm in the middle of it. No, wait, I *am* it. This cloud is me: I know it. Little Miss Bright

Ideas, I glow with the knowledge. Birds twitter and flutter not just about but *through* me.

Then I notice Eric at his bedroom window with a bit of a gloomy look. I flew up there like a sparkly angel on a mission, but he was okay: just staring out into the morning, watching things. His vibe was pretty calm as far as I could tell. I leant close and whispered, *I love you Eric, sorry I didn't make it last night.* Being in his physical body, of course, he couldn't exactly hear me, but a tiny smile appeared on his lips. Least it looked that way to me – one of those Mona Lisa smiles. Now maybe you're thinking hypocrite slut type thoughts, but I really felt that way. I made a point of never using those words with guys, but then I really felt it. Like my heart suddenly opened up and tiny birds flew out, singing – or something.

Eventually, he turned his chair away and began to get dressed for the day. That was none of my business so I flew away, off round the neighborhood again. Except for neighbor Nicole standing staring at what was likely her new koi carp, - it was. Mostly looking at stuff I never saw when alive, like roofs and chimneys and skylights. Lotta weird stuff on roofs, especially, like factories and stores and shit. Do people climb up there and leave it on purpose? They must, I can't see the wind blowing it up there. I mean all kinds of weird stuff that you can't even describe never mind figure out: rusty metal contraptions, curved, or maybe melted, plastic things, boxy stuff that was part cardboard and part wood and things that I've decided, after serious consultations in the student lounge, to call industrial enigmas.

Hours of fun that was. That's if you're into hours, which I'm kind of not. Not exactly girly stuff I know, but there you go, I never was a typical Barbie and hair gel type. For a while after that I followed cars about, kind of flying around them as they changed lanes and turned and stuff. Then I got bored and went back to good old Happydeadland. It was getting so I was, like, relieved to return. That was new. Maybe I was getting really to like it. Maybe it was going to be home after all.

17. Things Happen

Things happen. The dead do their stuff just like the living. Stuff to do, places to go, fun to be had. That thing called time, that you used to live by, passes. I immersed myself for a while, but enough of those earth agonies. Except for Eric: that I kept up. Felt like a sacred duty somehow. Normal boyfriends you could skip for a bit, but Eric, we're like soulmates. Mentioned this to Sonja and she'd said *Yeah, you've been tight before.* I had a sneaky suspicion she meant past lives and she nodded, *Sure.* I should've asked how she knew, but figured she was right on, she usually is. There's a place where you can check, I've heard in the lounge. Kinda mysterious, you know, one of those deeply rumored places.

Reminds me of that school cafeteria buzz about a dance club miles away where they supposedly handed out free E at the door. Raged for weeks. People I kinda trusted claimed they'd been and it was true. Turned out a local chemist boy whiz would show up on, like, I dunno, alternate Tuesdays and hand out the overflow from his latest batch. Wasn't even E – something real close though and certainly worth checking out. Or so I heard. Anyway, nobody died, and that's always a good sign. Night I finally wangled a ride there he wasn't around. Too bad, but we partied anyway.

Sonja suggested I check it out for myself. Sure I was intrigued, but I said I'd think about it. Figures though; Eric and I have been close ever since, what, grade three? Yeah that was when he helped me up after I'd slipped on some ice and hurt my butt on the way home. Up till then he'd just been some chubby boy in Mrs Clinton's class that looked at me funny during recess. I was kinda cute even then and had already learned the bitch brush off. But he was faithful and followed me about for a bit, enough that I got over my anti-boy stuff based on my psycho brothers and let him into the fold. The fold back then was Veronica, Leonore, Cindy, Cindy's twin brother Steven, and a couple of part-timers whose names I can't remember now. Not that it matters – this is grade three we're talking about. By grade five, everything had changed, but Eric was still there. We drifted apart in grade eight: puberty, pride, male bonding, the chess club? Some of each really. Plus I'd started on my who-will-I-be-today routine and I think he was kinda uncomfortable with the rotating personality syndrome. Looking back, I can see it must've been a challenge. I remember my mom saying, well no, shouting really, one day, *Mel, who the heck are you anyway? I don't even know anymore!*

By grade ten we were tight again. Like best friends who didn't need to see each other all the time, but who could call out of the blue and be instantly cool. And not just homework and hot gossip either – real stuff from the heart, sharing and trust and all that. He helped me out of a couple of jams I don't mind telling you. Details? Forget it. It'd bore you anyway. Typical teeny drama shit really. And the rest I think I've covered already.

Why I'm going on about Eric anyway? It was supposed to be stuff happening here in this chapter. Life in Happydeadland. Tell you one of the funny things: people, somebody, keeps changing the name on the sign at the edge of town. When I arrived and got my shit together enough to ask, Sonja took me over to look at it. A large, wooden square with hand carved letters that read 'Welcome to Essence'. I thought it sounded cool and we went on to other stuff. Next time I looked it said 'Welcome to Esse'. Next time 'Welcome to Spacey'. Then, 'Well Come'. Then, 'Well So'?

Pretty funny huh? So basically we have a no-name community. Or an all-name. And as far as I can tell no one cares. There's a lot of that here, the don't-worry-who-cares? routine. Not that people are destructive, more kind of playful anarchy type stuff. There's buildings that seem to change every time you look at them. It's happened so often I wonder if I'm seeing right. Course the buildings here are weird to begin with – like inventive weird; mainly because there's no limits with funding. There's no we-can't-afford-marble stuff here. And the marble you see, is it marble or some real good imitation? Who knows? I mean, this is marble that comes out of people's minds – mind marble, mind mahogany too. Architects just think about their design and it appears. I mean, they make plans first. And Sonja says they've got great mental control. And often they work together.

I've seen them, I know; standing in front of an empty space – a space between a games arcade and a beachwear shop. A sign had been up for a while so we knew something was coming. Did the sign keep changing? You bet. First time I noticed it said 'Something's Coming!' Later it said 'Something!' Then 'Some Come'. Then 'Come and Some Go'. So one time I'm going by on my way somewheres, can't remember where, and it doesn't really matter, and there's a group of maybe five people standing there, quiet and staring at the space. Three guys are standing around them, going *Shhh!* It's a pretty busy walkway where they're standing, but people seem to understand and get all quiet as they're passing. And some, like me, stop to watch. What can I tell you? A building slowly appears starting from the ground up. I watch, amazed. Guess if you've seen this a hundred times, as Sonja has, it's no big deal. But for me it's a first. Looks like an old-fashioned ice cream parlor kinda – big windows either side of a middle door. It's made of this shiny creamy smooth stone stuff that kinda sparkles and glows. Course a lot of stuff glows here, it's glowworld, amongst other things. And of course, with the amount of college-age stoners here, glowing is well, you know, accepted. It really is like being on mushrooms here – the glow, the buzz, the whisper – but I know you won't believe me, 'cause it's like a fantasy come true. Well Happydeadland is a fantasy come true, like all the best stuff you wanted suddenly all in place. I guess you'll just have to believe me till you get here yourself. But that's just like the bible anyway. People believe that till they get here. Why not some wacky wingnut teenage girl? I ask you. Or ask your best, recently dead, buddy when he comes to visit.

Anyway, the building's kind of assembling itself, just like it would in a cartoon, and the second floor's like one of those old English type houses – wooden beams with the stucco-y stuff between and windows with little squares in the glass – and it all leans out over the street. And then there's a third floor roof garden thing. What a hodge-podge, but a kinda cool hodge-podge. The word SMILE appears over the door with littler letters underneath: music-video-books-café. Cool! We need another place like that. We got at least one that I know of but it's always busy and you can't get a seat, and this one's way cozier and like, you know, European looking. The other one's this big square Yankee emporium thing, with like big video screens and dance area, which is cool but this will be different – attract a different crowd. Laugh if you want, but different crowds are as important here as where you live. Dead people are no more like cattle than live ones. We have our preferences, which leads me to the next thing I did that day.

When I came across the architects I was on my way to church. Yeah you heard right – church. There's a couple here. Well, at least four that I know of. And a synagogue and Koran place, what do they call them, temples? It's not a particularly religious place this, such a college-age party town, but they have the churches in case we get bored or freaked or something. Least that's the way it seems to me.

I'd met a few religious kids in my dorm building area, or at least they looked and acted that way. Some were just continuing on with the life they'd lead as kids with their parents without really knowing why, but then a lot of us are doing that, and some seemed like they were really onto something, like the existence of the afterlife proved what their bible predicted. This I picked up from shooting the breeze in one of the lounges. The shock of just arriving here kinda makes people more open than they'd usually be so there's lots of sharing going on, at least for a while.

Sonja had asked me a couple of times if I felt like religion would be something I'd be interested in. I'd said *Nah* a couple of times, not really sure of what I wanted but not ready to take that kind of step. But I guess I had some lingering something or others going, 'cause I kept thinking about going and checking it out. Okay, let's call it curiosity.

So I get to one of the churches. It's nicely set back with, like, lawns and gardens around it. A small empty parking lot. Funny thing about parking lots: we don't really need them here, but a lot of places have them – little ones just for the memory I think. People'd feel weird without them maybe. There's another one next to it, also with great landscaping going on, both kinda traditional looking. Small too, as if they weren't too hopeful about getting many visitors but were still ready to hang out the flag anyway.

Well wouldn't you know it; I meet the pastor's wife coming out, but it's actually the pastor herself. Liz, she tells me to call her. Fine with me. *How do ya do, I'm Mel.* I ask her if she gets many kids comin' around. She says quite a few, some to try it out, some to settle in, and some just to talk a bit. I tell her I'm probably only a talker but she says that's no problem; she's got all the time in the world now. Turns out she was a minister's wife on earth but died of cancer. *The Lord took me for a reason, and I think this is it.* She seems happy enough, so I guess she's adjusted and all. Like other church types I met on earth she seems to feel that everything in her life and now death has a reason, that none of it just, like, happened. I guess I don't get that. Seems to me stuff just happens and when people don't like what happened they have to figure out some reason why the shit hit the fan and when they figure out that reason, and sometimes it's God stuff, then they're happy about it, or adjusted or something. I say shit happens and you deal with it the best you can. What about earthquakes and floods and stuff I ask her, you think that's God's will? With all those people dying like that? She gives the God-works-in-mysterious-ways argument but with different words, more round about, like she's figuring it as she goes rather than reciting the party line, as my dad would say.

We sit on a bench by a flower garden and that seems so nice I forget what I wanna say next. But she's cool with that; she just sits and waits. After her spiel and me with nothing to say you'd think she'd jump on me to make a conversion at high speed, but no, she's just sitting there, cool and calm. The silence gets real comfortable for some reason. Well, there's birds chirping and a breeze on the trees and stuff, but it works out like a silence, kind of. You know, something you can settle into. Eventually we agree that this world, whatever it is, heaven or nearly heaven, is so great (Liz says *sublime*) just kind of being is all you need. That leads us into wondering how and why. Liz thinks it's God's gift to us after a lifetime of challenge and suffering. Like a reward? I ask. Well maybe, but maybe it's the next stage of growth. Like evolution, like adapting and stuff? Liz says she was thinking more blossoming than adapting. She's not sure Darwin had all the answers. I ask if she thinks the church has all the answers. Maybe it's the way I ask, like I won't take any shit, but she looks pensive for a moment before answering. As far as she's concerned Jesus has the answers not the church. Churches, she goes on, are like repositories of questioning faith, because all true faith is questioning, and they should be available to all seekers to either practice their faith or air their doubts. I bring up Mohammed and Buddha. Liz says she can't speak for them, although she met some very nice Buddhists and Muslims when she was alive. Her husband initiated some interfaith dialogues in their community and they were still ongoing when she passed. In fact, people of several faiths attended her funeral and she could feel all their goodwill and prayers. She really felt blessed.

I know what she means, the funeral vibe was really strong for me, nearly too much. What about wars and shit, where do all those religious guys in the White House get off starting wars like they do? I mean what's Christian about that? Liz comes on with the judge-not-that-ye-be-not-judged stuff and says they must have known things they couldn't tell us. I tell her about my granny, the 75 year old peace activist, and what she would say to that. She laughs and says she must be Democrat. I give her Gran's line: *The Democrats are too stupid to be corrupt and The Republicans are too stupid to be anything but corrupt*. She laughs even harder and then tells me she prefers to stay out of politics altogether as it only makes people angry with each other. I see that for what it is, one of those get-me-off-the-hook remarks, but don't push her on it. Despite my feisty bitch pose I've still got touches of what-do-I-know-I'm-just-a-kid in me.

Then I ask if she's changed her religious views since dying. Yeah is the answer, but she is still in the process and if she's really honest with herself her views were in a constant state of mutation on earth too. 'Mutate' always makes me think of viruses, but I stay with the program and ask which views exactly. She was never really sure that heaven was a place – kinda figured it for a state of mind more than anything. Well now she can see it is a place, although there's heavens and heavens and how this one rates she's not sure. Plus she's seen plenty of non-Christians here, so that kinda puts your faith to the test. She knows a lot of people who'll have a hard time with that when they get here – if they get here instead of somewhere else. Then she asks what views of mine changed.

Interesting question that. First off, I wonder what views I had exactly. All that gloomy gothgirl stuff; it was more like abstaining from life than indulging in death. It was like being too cool to live, least that's the way it looks now. I guess I thought death was something between an escape and a long sleep. Liz asks if I know about the sleepers. I say *no, who are they?* All the Christians who believed that they would sleep till judgment day. They're all in like, hospital type places she says: thousands of them, maybe more. She knows 'cause she got the tour. Just like endless rows and wards with people sleeping and one or two folk keeping an eye on them in case anyone wakes up, which once in a while, someone does. *Sounds kind of sad,* I say. *It is,* she says. They could be having a life, a good life at that.

I'd never really thought out my escape and long sleep options I tell her, they were just ideas, notions, whatever. Like angels and harps and saints floating about seemed cracked and nothingness seemed like such a waste. She asks me if I ever heard that Woody Allen joke about eternal nothingness being okay just as long as you were dressed for it. I haven't and it's weird 'cause Eric was a big Woody fan and had most of the videos. We did a pretty good version of that scene from *Annie Hall* with the lobsters loose in the kitchen. Liz says she doesn't know the movies well, but her husband Dan told her. And she thinks somebody told him.

I ask if she still believes in Jesus. Why, of course she does. Why would dying change that? She looks genuinely puzzled. I ask if she's seen him around. Sure, she attended a service where he made an appearance. I imagine him stepping up to take a bow sometime after the sermon, after Liz says, *And here's the man you've all been waiting for,* but know it's a crock. She describes an open air festival kind of service, with what sounds like thousands of people, all looking up. And at a certain point, He appears floating way above everyone, smiling and raising his hand in greeting. The feeling that went through the crowd was amazing. Absolutely blissful, a blessing you could feel massaging your heart. She was crying and hugging the person next to her. Many were on their knees, with the adoration or praise in their eyes and others were weeping uncontrollably and had to be helped away. And you know what, he looked different to everyone. Talking later she encountered so many variations on the vision. Some saw Jesus, some saw a blinding light, some saw him surrounded by angels, others thought they recognized some of the disciples there and debated about which ones. Others were, like, shocked into silence and quickly left, as if they couldn't handle the intense emotions, which, she had to admit, verged on hysteria.

I asked if he actually said anything. *He spoke to our hearts Mel, you had to be there. I'll let you know of his next visit if you like.* Well, who could snub an invite like that? Makes a date with Bono look pretty tame. Of course I said yes. How could I say anything else? Besides it didn't look like a cult or anything. So we discussed this talking straight to your heart thing. It's like a direct communication without words. *So that's like love,* I said. *Yeah,* she said, *but a very precise kind of love, like a well-aimed dart to your heart.* I told her about the love I felt for Eric and how guilty I felt for being, you know, this happy girl in heaven while he gets to struggle with being crippled every day. Liz said maybe he feels guilty for me being dead while he's still alive. I told her about meeting up with him when he was asleep and out of his body. She thought that was wonderful of me, to be so dedicated to another's welfare, but wondered if it wouldn't be better for him in the long run if I was to pull away. That felt like leaving him stranded; no, I didn't think I could do that. I didn't mention the sex as I figured she'd disapprove. She was cool, but not that cool.

I ask if she didn't go visit her husband when he was sleeping. Well he just slept so there was really not much point, although she did pray for his health and happiness while she was in his bedroom. Then she started to sob a little and I said I was sorry to have brought it up. Turns out he's not always in his bedroom. He's courting another woman and sometimes spends the weekend at her house. Of course he needs a helpmate in his ministry, she knows that, but she can't help herself. She knows it's selfish and she's prayed for strength to cope.

So there I am, putting my arm around her shoulder, trying to comfort her. She's not as bad as my mom, so it's a bit easier that way. With my mom I'm this useless ghost girl that can't do much. At least here, with us both dead, we can relate. She comes around eventually and wants to show me around the church.

It's just kind of a church church, if you know what I mean, nothing special that I could see. But I was polite and nodded and smiled at all the right places. My gran taught me that. She said if you nodded and smiled at all the right places people would never know you were bored and you could escape all the faster. Have to say though, Liz was as nice a person as you could hope to meet, and I really hoped we could be friends and stuff. She said sure and gave me a hug that felt, you know, real, and not like she was just going through the motions to get me signed up for her religion. We sat down and discussed the relationship thing again. I brought it up really. For myself at first, but then I saw it was more for her. She really needed to like, vent about this other woman her husband was spending the odd weekend with. See it was his old girlfriend before they got married. And she was something religious too, but a different, what do they say, denomination? She was mad at him for doing it, mad at her for, like, plotting the whole thing, and mad at herself for being mad 'cause it's not, like, the proper Christian thing to do. You're supposed to be forgiving and compassionate and stuff.

I say, feel what you feel and be proud of it. There's way too much feeling stuff and lying about it. At least there was on earth. Maybe not so much here. Trying to pretend certain feelings aren't there is stupid and makes you sick if you ask me. My mom's a perfect example; way too busy being nice for the neighbors – neighbors she could happily strangle sometimes. Anyway, Liz kinda opened up about this and I think it did her a lot of good. She'll forgive someday, I know she will. It's just a matter of time, although like I say there's not really any time here. I didn't tell her about Grant, though I was sorely tempted; got some guilt about that for sure. But it's more important I'm there for Eric when he needs me than bothering him with my guilt crap. Why does he need that? I'm a creature of impulse and I'll never change. I know, never say never.

Anyway, I did leave eventually, and Liz is pretty much my new best friend. She's not much of a party girl, but I'll get her dancing one day, I know I will. Just give me time. Walking back through town I noticed people sitting in the new place already, licking ice creams and sipping lattes. We do stuff fast here, I tell ya.

18. The End of Avoidance

So after a while, a few days as far as you earth types are concerned – although I don't know where I get the confidence to say that, Miss Afterlife Knowledge.com herself – I reach the end of avoidance. That's after amusing myself with every little thing on the way. Eventually, as I always knew I would, I go back to the family – with way more reluctance than love I can tell ya. I didn't even bring it up with Sonja 'cause I felt a lecture coming on. Oh it wouldn't be a lecture to her, she's so kind and understanding and helpful, but it would sound like one to me, in the state I'm in, kind of hyper toxic sibling sensitivity. Turns out my darling brother had internet porn stuff on his computer, or they thought he had some kiddy stuff, but the girls just looked young they weren't actually, but of course they open it up and there's his stash right there, way too much to pass over, and they're throwing the dealer charge at him. Where else did that roll of fifties come from? And they're doing their best to roll Todd into it all, but no evidence so far. I'll bet he flushed his instantly, or else passed it to Mike somehow. They were all dealing as far as I knew. I never got on their case 'cause I did so much myself. Plus I can't say I honestly cared for the little shits that much anyway.

As you can guess my parents are, like, terminally wired over all this. And I thought my mom was in a mess over me. Course dad arranged bail in a few hours. Darren's got his life back for now and looks pretty pleased with himself – well, when he's with his buds anyway. At home he's quiet, polite and responsible. I watched him wash the dinner dishes and help my mom with some stuff and couldn't believe it. Even got his hair neatly trimmed. None of that dorky doofus shit we used to get – all grown up now. But I watched him – well you know, followed him, like us dead people can do – and when he got to one of his friend's apartments, well it was one different Darren: Mr Cool with a can of brew and a batch of boy chuckles for the band of brothers assembled in his honor. I left; I couldn't take it. Guy's a creep, always was.

Checked in on dad. Just thought of him and wondered where. Suddenly I'm at Andrea's. They're drinking coffee at her kitchen table and looking serious. Oh, I get it; dad's explaining how he can't move out like they'd planned. Bad enough me dying, but all this legal stuff, he's worried about my mom's ability to cope right then. Andrea agrees, and, like, really seems to support him. God she's nice. I really hope they're able to get together one day. I think they'd make a good couple. I'm sure Mom would meet someone else. I mean she's got her faults and all but a lot of guys really like her. Dinner parties and barbeques at our place, there was always some guy, maybe a friend, a neighbor, or one of Dad's clients, but I'd always see the admiring looks comin' her way when she wasn't noticing. She's no great looker, but she's got this kind, care-about-you attitude that people always notice – especially guys. She always thought she was fat, and while she's not exactly slimbabe, she's still got, like, curves in all the right places.

Then it looks like they're gonna get friendly, so I disappear pronto. Not really ready for that. And let's face it, it's like really rude. I know what you're thinking, where do I draw the line between a couple drinking coffee and talking and a couple getting it on? I dunno, I just draw it, like everyone does, like you'd do if you were here. Then I can't decide what to do, so I fly around the streets. Flying's always fun; dodging around people and cars like some crazy bird. You know how birds will fly up past your windshield, right at the very last second, as if they're, like, dancing with death? Well, I can do that shit no problem. Takes some practice, sure. And you gotta set yourself some rules, like not touching or part way going through windshields, because as a ghost you can go part way through real easy. So the rule is just to skim the glass but not touch it. But flying *under* cars as they pass, that's the biggie for me. Took a lotta nerve to begin with. I always panicked at the last minute and held back. Don't know why, stupid really when you can fly right through the thing no problem – one more thing you'll love when you get here, all you wannabe daredevils.

After a while I wonder about mom. The thought leads me straight to some theatre somewhere. She and Nicole and some other lady I don't know are watching some play and laughing. Well that's good; I'm glad. I kind of hover there for a bit, taking in the show and the audience. It's way into the middle of the thing and I can't really figure out what's happening. I mean, like, the story. For no particular reason I decide to fly up to the Arctic – really just to see what it's like – so I give myself the command, go north. And away we go. I'm over the Great Lakes, one of them anyway, in no time, and boy is it ever beautiful – just like a big sea really, although I guess there's differences if you really get into it. Then Canada I guess. It looks just like the States as far as I can see. You know, cities and then suburbs and then like fields and some forests and hills and stuff. Why'd I think it'd be any different? More forests and lakes as I go north, miles and miles of them. I start to wonder if they're ever gonna end. No people anywhere. I feel like I'm getting lost. After, like, ages, it gets all flat and boring. This must be the tundra. Then it's white with snow and then it's like nothing but snow no matter where you look – weird, but weirdly beautiful. I don't know whether to lie on the snow and look at the sky or float up there and gaze down at all the snow. I do some of both. You know me, like to be fair. It's amazing, it really is, but I get to feeling lonely. It's spooky out here in the middle of this white nowhere. No funny lookin' penguins or dancing bears to liven things up either.

I've got this vague notion that there's a lesson for me here, but I can't wait to find out what it is. I think about Eric and like magic there I am in his bedroom, watching him tap, tap away at his keyboard. I park myself on the floor opposite and just bask in his dedicated vibe. He's working on something, an essay for class maybe. In a way he looks just like he always did. Course that's 'cause he's sitting down, but still, it's something – something to hang on to? Well, I guess.

It feels like it'll be a while till he sleeps and comes over, but I'm happy to wait, especially after that lonesome jag in the Arctic. Wow, that was weird. In the interval I recall what Liz said about him maybe feeling guilty, you know, for me being dead. I tell you one thing; his family life is way better: parents happy together, one really nice sister who's training to be a vet. Mom's a fish fanatic; got this huge aquarium in the front room, and I mean huge. They all sit and stare at it after dinner, like it's a TV. Don't laugh; I used to myself when I came over for dinner. Dad's some kind of engineer; always got blueprints spread out on the desk in his office. And they all get along! It's too funny. They're probably the best kind of family to cope with his problem. I wonder if he feels a guilty having such a nice supportive family while mine's falling apart at the seams – he might. I have spilled the details.

I notice he's finished work and is looking at some website. Probably politics, he's a junkie for that – knows all the conspiracy stuff backwards: talks circles around me, which takes some doing let me tell ya. Curious for some reason, I take a peek. Hmm, it's some stuff about dead people. That's something I should know about. I move closer, almost breathing on his neck. Yup, it's some kind of communication from the land of the dead. Holy shit, it's those 9/11 people, or some of them.

That happened not long after my crash, so I was, like, completely clued out for ages. When I started talking to Eric when he was OBE, that's when I found out. No, wait a minute, somebody told me before that, but I kinda put it out of my mind. I didn't know you could watch earth TV then either. Let's face it, after I got settled I just wanted to party. And the people I hung with were the same: just amazed to be still alive and to not have to fight for your right to party. And if everyone came here or nearby when they died who really cared how they got here? What was the point? I sat back on the floor and rested. Eric would be sleeping sometime soon. I'd talk with him then.

And I did. We were, umm, intimate first, and then he told me about this website he just discovered – these 9/11 people that lived together in a village on the astral plane. That was where I lived, right? Had I met them? Could I? I reminded him that it was, like, really vast, the spirit world, way bigger than the world. I said it with confidence, which is weird, 'cause it's basically just what Sonja told me. But she's pretty reliable anyway. Did he know where it was? Like did the site specify? No, it didn't. And nobody was saying their name or anything – something to do with not upsetting their families. What about the Flying Mohammeds he says, where the heck are they? Well, shit, what about Muslim Heaven, that'd be my guess. He's got that conspiracy look in his eyes, so I know he's gonna say something about some secret agency hidden deep within some other slightly-less-secret agency remote-controlling the planes from some bunker deep within the Rockies, or some basement deep within the Bronx. He's a bit off the wall when it gets to this stuff and I can't say I'm with him all the way, but you don't think those two dopey white guys did that Oklahoma thing all by themselves do ya, the Ryder truck boys? Just about everyone that worked at that sleasebag motel said they seen Middle-Eastern guys with them the whole week previous. How come the FBI didn't interview *them*? As Eric loves to say, there's something rotten in the state of Denmark.

Eric tells me these people seem pretty messed up. Like why them and why now? Like as if wrong place, wrong time wasn't good enough for them. They're living in this village together just 'cause they all died on the same day – all different types of people, from major businessmen types to secretaries and janitors and firemen, and you know, people just dropping off packages and shit: different religions too – people who thought the afterlife was just for Catholics and people who didn't believe in an afterlife at all. I said hey, I was surprised too, I thought it was just for U2 fans and the better class of stoners. Just kidding. Anyway, I promise to check it all out and get back to him. That seems to smooth his feathers. We get so wrapped up in this stuff I never actually tell him about Liz, the lady minister, and her church and seeing Jesus and all that. Funny, you'd think that'd be the first thing I'd tell him – another time maybe. No, another time for sure.

And believe it or not I did check it out. You can't say I'm not a woman of my word. I asked Sonja next time I saw her, which was pretty soon actually, and of course she knew. What's her line, umm, people in my line of work need to be kept abreast of the latest? Yeah something like that. In your world someone shows you how to get somewhere or gives you directions, but here they just kind of take you there. We switched levels so fast I'm not even sure we switched levels. Going up or down or going across, if you do it quick enough you can't tell the difference – least I can't.

So I'm on the edge of this town, standing in a field, or maybe a meadow – that sounds nicer doesn't it – wild flowers, all lovely and different, kind of nodding their little heads in a breeze you can hardly feel. Across the grass I can see a group of, like, stacked condos like you might see in Florida or southern California: kinda cubey with second floor balconies and stucco-y. I remember seeing hotel rooms near the beach once like them. Where were we? Aruba? Maui? Can't remember. Family holidays all kind of blend together now. I see now I had this guilty trip going on over them. Some kids in my school never got to go farther than Cape Cod and I was all over 'cause Dad had a good job. Never did think much of it then. Here I am on the edge of this village of 9/11 survivors, about to go in and talk to them for Eric's sake – I don't care that much myself, I mean we're all dead here, and lots through violence and trauma and shit – and I start thinking about my family holidays when I was like ten or eleven, and feeling guilty about them. Gees, I really pick the times, don't I? I always used to say, back in the earth days, hangin' out, shootin' the cool teen breeze with the gang, that I wasn't gonna do crack just to really feel that ghetto vibe, and now I wonder what was pushin' me when I said that. Enough; I'm off to do my research.

First person I meet is just coming out her front door as I pass. I say *Hello* and she looks at me a bit suspicious and then apologizes. Apparently a lot of strangers have been comin' by and they feel like specimens in a zoo, on top of the fact that they're mostly still freaked out about the whole disaster thing. As she goes on it sounds more like a life, the universe and everything rant, just on the edge of what the heck was God thinking about anyway? I've heard a lot of that around here already so I recognize the signs.

She asks where I live and I describe it to her. She says that it sounds really great and that she'd like to see it sometime. I said no problem. I tell her it's pretty cool spot they got here – windy walkways and plants and little trees everywhere. I look up and see like a long ivy plant trailing over a balcony with flower pots sitting on it. I can see an elbow and a forearm and imagine a conversation and drinks. Not only is it a couple of her neighbors, it's a couple she used to work with. She surprised that they're still friends after what they went through. Then she changes the subject as if she's opened a can of worms and wants it shut again. She's going to their sidewalk café for a latte; did I want to come along? When I tell her that me and lattes are like this, she laughs and says *Yeah some things never change*. Her name is Cassie, she says, holding out her hand. I shake it and we walk away.

At the café – just a few chairs and little round tables set outside a storefront really – about five or six locals are chewing the fat, and looking like they're expecting, any minute now, to get caught relaxing. Is it that too-good-to-be-true vibe I've seen so often at my own holiday camp? Nah, it's a bit more shifty-eyed even, like they're sure the shit's gonna hit the fan any minute, and they're figuring on an escape route or at least a set of excuses. I'm wondering if it's leftover anxiety when Cassie introduces me around. Everyone is smiley and friendly. Hey, I'm pretty good at that myself sometimes and this is one of those times. I tell you; I'd have been perfect cheerleader material if I hadn't also been such a rebel stoner chickaroo as well.

I'm doing such a good job of being Melanie right now it's like I'm standing aside and watching me do it. Watching the robot I used to call it, back in the old days. This time is, like, really vivid; I'm actually, somehow, looking down on myself from above, like my very own little guardian angel. Being your own guardian angel, now isn't that weird? There I am, doing the social thing. How clever of me! It's just a few seconds in all, but what a feeling, wow! And nobody seems to notice. They're all too busy being themselves.

Somebody asks how I got here and I launch into the story and the whole thing about Eric. Murmurs of sympathy as I talk. Maybe because they're all older than me, or at least they look older – kind of 30 to 35 I'd guess. When I'm done and though with the questions a guy called Matt says *Well, I guess you know how we all got here.*

Well, says Melanie, *Kinda, I just got the headlines really.*

Well, he says, *we got people here from the planes and the buildings: firemen, cops, janitors, you name it. Some of us were brought here; some of us woke up in beds here; some of us came to on the fields outside town. A lot of us are still in some kind of shock. Folks you see here are the more sociable ones, others stay in their apartments, you know, keeping to themselves till they work it all out.*

Another woman joins in and says *We came here so suddenly, so without any kind of warning, it's very hard to accept and adjust. There's this inability to believe it actually happened at all. Seems like a bad dream really. Some of us think we're still going to wake up and go back to work like nothing happened.*

The guy spoke again. *It's hard for us to get used to not having anything to do anymore. There's not much, you know, business to transact here. Some turn to their hobbies: reading, playing cards, that type of thing.*

TV? I asked.

Yeah sure, it's hard to give up. And some don't want to.

It's like their link to the old life, the woman said.

I said some stuff about the kids I was around and how they coped or didn't cope. I said the ones that coped the best were the ones who'd suffered long and slow from something like cancer. They were so happy to be finally free, while the ones, like me, who died quickly without warning, were the most screwed up. No, I wasn't that screwed up myself, least I didn't think so, but if this shit with my family got any worse I could go right off the deep end, wherever that was. Everyone laughed.

I felt great. I was the center of attention and I was doing just fine. Shit, I could have my own TV show carryin' on like this: interviewing people about their deaths and stuff. Sound good? Why not?

We kinda went on like this for a bit, swapping stories and that sort of thing. Some architect guys had thought up their little condo development when they got here, kinda just for them – Instant buildings, what a trip that had been. Course they didn't use the word trip. That's from watchin' Eric's DVD of *Gimme Shelter* too many times – that and *Bummer man*. Eric loves that old hippy lingo. My dad does too; he won't admit it, but three drinks and CSNY singing *Ohio* or *Wooden Ships*'ll bring tears to his eyes every time. Mom was nuts about that song *Guinevere*. I asked them once what living in America was like in 1970. They got all tongue-tied right away. Dad said you really had to be there. Mom agreed and reminded me that was the year of her long trip to Hawaii, which was pretty much like another world. It was a cop out and I let them away with it.

It's a small thing I guess, but I wish I hadn't. Regrets, I know, what good are they, and that's as true here as there. Least I think it is.

Of course I'm wandering, don't I always? Anyway, I hung out for a whiles longer, then figuring I'd split before outstaying my welcome, I made my bye-byes. They all said to come back again whenever. I said sure. I walked past the town edge and into the fields before clicking out of their world and back into mine. I just imagined my place and said I wanted to be there *now!* and there I was walking up to the front doors of the dorm.

19. The Following Chapter

Are you getting all this? I mean, I'm trying to make it straightforward and easy to take in, but this sentence from school keeps coming up: *Trying to impose a narrative pattern on the chaos of life*. I forget what we were studying now, some book but which one? *On the Road*? I suppose I don't care that much, I mean that theory stuff never did get to me, I just liked the writing and reading part. And I did like *On the Road* and that other one, umm, *The Dharma Bums*? Don't know whether it was the lifestyle thing, the writing that was like breathing and running and jumping or the love for that wild, out there America that can't be put in boxes and governed. Did Kerouac actually say that or am I just imagining it? There's another guy I could probably see if I had the courage. Sonja says most of them, the famous dead ones, writers and film stars and what not, are all here somewhere, if you really want to check them out. Lots of them still do concerts and stuff. She says she's seen Frank Sinatra and Elvis Presley and some jazz guys I can't remember. Kurt's not doing anything like that, said he wasn't ready.

See, that's where this imposing a narrative pattern on the chaos of life comes in. Look at the chaos of my life and mind. I can't keep my mind on anything for more than a minute – not even that sometimes. I know what you're saying: It's the drugs; she warped her brain with drugs. But I was like this when I was twelve and, like, totally straight. Mom would say how can a scatterbrain be so smart? Because my marks were always good, and she was right, most days I couldn't find a pair of socks that matched. Then, at fourteen, I turn into this bohemian fashion queen, scouring all the downtown bargain shops for out-there outfits and Mom's like, half-amazed and half oh-my-god-that's-my-daughter.

Was there a narrative to my life? And was it imposed on the

chaos? Maybe that's what my mom's trying to do now: make a story out of my life, a story she can tell the grandkids. Oh my god, doesn't that make you think? My little shit brothers are gonna have kids one day – never thought of that. Will I be like a legend to them? Their maiden aunt cut down in the flower of youth? If my mom has anything to do with it I will. Don't know if I want to be someone's long lost maiden aunt either. And now that I'm here in Happydeadland, that narrative would be continued here. It's like the last half; first half is Mel in America, second is Mel in Heaven. That's if Happydeadland is actually heaven, and not some kind of, oh I don't know, substitute for those not-quite-holy-enough to get into the real place. Except they don't tell us 'cause they don't want you to know you're missing out. Maybe that's just paranoid. Sonja would think it was. She says there's all kind of heavens, and they're filled with folk who think their heaven is the only heaven.

I've been thinking about this for a while now and I want you to know about it. The life you're living there, on earth – the one most of you think is the real one and a lot of you think is the only one – well it's really only the first half. I'm getting more and more sure of that. I know you're probably thinking she's young she's got most of her life to live, and you're right, but I've met people who were old when they died and they've got a whole new life here just like us kids. Sonja was fifty-three when she came here and now she looks about twenty-eight. And a bunch of the teachers here say much the same – they all look about thirty-ish and really, you know, prime-of-life healthy. My dulcimer guy, Eugene, says he was seventy-eight when he died and really looked his age. Died in '92 after a stroke; played lots of guitar and dulcimer for years, but not like in a famous way, just amateur stuff and teaching young people a couple of evenings a week. Said he was some kind of an office manager for, like, forever. He also plays this little harp nicely, though he's not like confident enough to teach it. But he said if anyone wants to learn he knows a lady nearby who'll take on a few students. It's called a Celtic harp and he says it's mainly for Irish folk music. I'm thinking of going by; it's got such a great sound but it looks way more complicated than the dulcimer which is hard enough for me.

You know when I was this teen writer girl back on earth, that first half I was talking about there, writing my gloomy gothy stories and freakin' out my friends, I never thought I'd be putting something like this together now (now as in here and now in Happydeadland). Well, who would? But it's the best thing I've done, no question. It's me for real even if you think this is all, like, not for real. Too bad it's just on tape. Well it's not tape, it's like a computer disc or something, and when I'm done I'm gonna put it in a computer and it just, like, prints out – or so they tell me. Then what'll I do with it? Love to get it out and about in the earth world, but how do you do that from here? Sonja tells me you still have to make an arrangement with someone there who wants to help. Help by taking dictation. You put thoughts and words into their head and they write it down. But they're not gonna always get it exactly right, even if they're trying real hard. Or you kinda put your hand on top of theirs and they relax and let you write. Sonja says it takes a bit of practice but if you can get used to it, both of you, it's the more accurate way.

Seems to me like Andrea would be the best bet; she's like way more ready to communicate and stuff. But it would take a really long time I think, you know, to get it all down correctly. Let's face it; it's a heck of a thing to ask someone. I guess I'll ask her sometime. I wonder what she'd say. I mean, when you think of it it's a pretty weird request. And would she remember later, or would she get some garbled thing about writing, but writing what exactly? Oh, who knows, I sure don't.

I guess I'm still a mixture of knows and don't knows. I mean, this second half of your life thing I was talking about earlier, I'm pretty sure about that. And to even get that, if you think about it, is pretty radical. Seen a guy the other day with a t-shirt that said *Yup, there's an afterlife alright, so what?* There's a lot of that here, this feeling that, Yeah okay, we're here, now what? That's where some of the kids wind up at churches and what not. Then they'll sit around the lounges and go over what they've come up with. Sometimes one of the party crowd will sit in, but either joke around like it's stupid or get bored and get up and leave. There's also these little meetings they go to – one's called Eckankar (I know 'cause I wrote it down) – that aren't exactly church religion things but you can see they're trying to offer answers. So on that stuff I'm a don't-know, but maybe hanging out with Liz will change that. But I get the feeling – don't know why – that I'm more there for Liz than she's there for me. Sounds arrogant I guess for a little chick like me, but like I said way back when, teens do have something to say: something worth listening to. That brings up another issue: longer you're here the less you feel like a teen. Less you feel like yourself really. Sonja says I'm growing with the experience and I guess she's right, but it feels like growing in a different way than if I was still on earth and going to college there, although how I can make the comparison I don't know. Oh, it's all too weird, there's so much happening, and trying to keep track of it all, I don't know why I bother; I could be just living and having fun like most everyone else, but no I'm cursed with thinking about it all, like I gotta personally solve all the issues. Even Sonja says I sweat over too much. *Forget all this meaning of life stuff, Mel. Just live and love,* she says. Sounds good, doesn't it? And mostly I do that, I go from one thing to another, trying not to torture myself with the big why, but every once in a while you can't hold back. It's all so amazing, or amazingly weird. I mean, here we all are, dead, and life just goes on like nothing happened – or not much.

Grant told me about a concert he was at somewheres – not here. One of his guides took him. It was like about half those guys, the dead ones, from the Grateful Dead and some of their dead friends – a big, open air concert: megafans dancing away like it was Woodstock all over again. I forget their names, but you know who I'm talking about don't ya? Anyway, they called themselves The Living Dead and Grant said they were hot, fans goin' nuts, the whole nine yards. He couldn't really believe it; it was like being in a movie for him.

But you see what I mean, don't you? All these dead people having fun just like nothing happened, it's just too weird sometimes. Eventually you just force yourself to stop thinking about it. You see it's not doin' you any good. I've heard other kids say that it's just like when they were alive on earth. They'd drive themselves crazy, sittin' in their room trying to figure out the meaning of it all and then give up 'cause it wasn't getting them anywhere. One guy said it was like lacerating yourself, and if you know about teens and knives, you'll see the point of that.

So maybe I should just say here is like there, 'cause most everyone who's not, like, brain dead, is still puzzling over the mystery of it all. There's no sudden like *Oh yeah, now I get it* thing going on. Well for some people it's bit like that, but it doesn't usually last: sometimes because the initial thrill of not actually being dead and gone kinda fades with time, and sometimes because they soon discover it's not just people from their religion that's sitting next to them at lunch. And sure, there's a few who never seem to get over missing the folks back home. I always think they're resisting having fun, like self-condemned to the gloomies, but Sonja says to just give 'em time, that they'll come around. Maybe she's right; she usually is. Maybe I'll just let Sonja impose the narrative, that way I can opt out for the chaos any time I feel like it. Just like a teen, right?

20. Reading the Newspaper

About three days have gone by earth time. I know 'cause I figured out that I can, like, zero in on the newspaper Dad's reading on his morning break. Seems like a funny way to keep track, and you might wonder why I'd bother anyway, but the ups and downs of these family dramas keep us dead kids on the hop up here. Not just me either: I talk about it with other kids so I know how they're coping. One girl, somebody I only just met – another Jennifer, there must be a hundred of them here – told me she was, like, obsessed with her younger sister's pregnancy. Girl's only fifteen and she thinks she should, like, put an end to it, but their parents are dragging it out, making her think it over, all that you-got-options talk, which if they were fifteen, they'd see they weren't so hot, then of course, you're into second trimester and things are pretty much settled. The adults get their way and the kids get to obey and be grateful. *Grateful for what?* Jen says. *A kid you don't want? A kid that winds up with some rich yuppie career-babe power-bitch too driven to drop her pants once in a while?* Maybe that's over doing it a bit, but I don't know about you, but I can see her point. Seems to me if you can't see her point you ain't been a teen lately.

But then maybe I'm wrong, 'cause I can think of one chick I met who was quite the opposite. She was pregnant and so deeply conflicted over it (that's her words not mine) she jumped off some bridge somewhere. Said she was too ashamed to live – didn't deserve to live. No surprise that she's from one of those churches where if you do anything wrong you're dead meat. What's that thing they do? Umm, she called it shunning I think. That's where they all pretend you're invisible, even as you're crying in the corner, like she was when she told me all this. And it was like years before. She'd spent, oh I dunno, ages in some yucky place where people were not just mean to her, but mean to each other, like all the time, like a way of life. Felt like hell but didn't fit the description somehow. I said, trying to cheer her up, *Sounds like the lobby on the way in to hell.* She grinned sort of. Anyway, she stayed put till some guide got her outta there – someone that sounded so much like Sonja I asked her name, but it was something else.

So now she's kinda settled here, for a while anyway, she's this serious studygirl, taking courses in just about everything you can think of and like, totally in a religious turmoil. It goes like this: she's still totally in love with Jesus, thinks most of the bible is true and not just stories, but figures God is way more merciful than her church made out. She's also got this thing about sin, that it's mistakes you make on the way to finding the right path. Anyway, she's got a sister too – a pregnant one who wants to terminate and she's, like, frantically trying to whisper in her ear about keeping it.

One guy I met dancing told me he'd already given up trying to keep his parents from bruising each other. *Pretty dysfunctional huh?* says I.

You bet, says he. *Got my sister out though. Grandparents took her* (this with a bit of a victorious grin). He didn't die from violence though – meningitis after a school dance. Still misses his girlfriend although he's got a new one here.

So you see what I mean about keeping us on the hop? Some days it seems like everyone's got their issues. And then some days it seems like everyone you run into is some kind of butterfly, just happy to flip from flower to flower. Heck some days I feel like that myself, or maybe it's just the fluttery way I think and talk.

So, back to three days have gone by; Dad's having a coffee at work, scanning his newspaper, although he's really thinking about some client's case. You see, I figured on how to read his thoughts, or at least some of them. Then he's onto all the family crisis stuff: starts with me dying and just goes downhill from there – regrets, guilt, all that good stuff. I say to him, really concentrating this time, like Sonja explained, *Don't feel bad. I'm right here with you and I love you just as much as I ever did.* Wow, that's a mouthful for old rebel Mel. Anyway, he lights up with a smile, just like's he's heard. Then his phone rings and he's in lawyer mode instantly. But he heard me, I know he did.

Then I flip over, on the wings of thought as Sonja likes to say, to see Mom. She's driving back from driving my useless brother to work: a CD/DVD distribution place, like a big warehouse really and just the spot to hide a few of his scams. I bet he's got stuff stashed all over. Not that I care much. Who would? Anyway, she seems okay, you know, coping, like she's fortified herself somehow, like she knows that she just can't keep on breaking down like she was when it was just me she had to worry about. That makes me feel good and uneasy at the same time. Uneasy is the jealous sibling trip for sure, and I can give you an hour of squealing over why I'm more worthy of my mother's anxiety than my brothers. But, hey, you've heard enough of that already; I wouldn't want to tip you into their side with lashings of chick-rant. As dad used to tell me when I was about to fly with rage, *That would be counter-productive.*

Mom stopped at a grocery store and I followed her around a bit as she picked out her stuff for the week. Don't know why really, think it just felt good to be with her and see she was doing okay. There was a tense moment though, when she stopped in front of my favorite yogurt, hesitated, and felt like a big dose of sad was about to swamp her. I tried to do that same thing I did with dad, and wow, it worked. She gave out a little smile and walked on. I tried to figure what I'd done right this time, because usually I'd get nowhere and she'd be in a sobbing heap on the couch or the bed. I think the trick is to not get upset or pissed in any way, but to, like, coolly decide what to do and stick with the program – like take the thought and push it into their thoughts without getting caught in their sloshy stuff. Like not be cruel-to-be-kind but being cool-to-be-kind. Yeah, that's it, cool to be kind.

So that was working pretty well and we got back in her car and drove off. We see Nicole as she's unpacking in the driveway and are invited in for coffee, least Mom is; I'm the invisible sidekick. It's kinda fun watching the ladies do the chat thing. I say ladies 'cause Nicole's friend Martha's there already. I can see myself being just like them if I'd stayed on earth, survived college and did the marriage/baby thing – not regret exactly, more like recognizing potential. Always figured I had potential, just didn't know what for, and suburban housewife chick was not one of the options on the table – not back then. But these three are trying their darnest to have fun, and you know what, they're doing a not half bad job. Survivors, that's what they are. What I'd be if I'd been through what they've been through. Nicole and Martha have had their own dose of shit and you know about my mom. I feel all proud and grown up just thinking about this.

I watch some more, all pleased with myself, and then think about Granny, who I haven't thought about in ages. Don't know why, other than she was always able to look after herself. She's at home, tidying up by the looks of things. Well, that's nice. Granny was always the shit disturber in the family, you never thought of her doing stuff like cleaning and cooking. She was always on committees, circulating petitions and making plans. And coming from her background, kinda privileged, she knew senators and governors and what not and was always on their cases for one thing or another. She said to me once, when I asked, *I push myself to the edge of the social register but never quite off, oh no, I'd never do that.* Anyway, here she is tidying up, and dusting for God's sake. I feel like telling her there's no dusting where I live, but it seems kinda dumb. No politics either and that would likely bother her some – likes her politics, that's for sure. That is maybe not quite right; it's not like I know everything or have been everywhere, but what I've done and where I've been tells me there's no political stuff going on. Who runs the place, I bet you'd ask if you had the chance, and I can more or less understand why. Even the college doesn't have much of an administration – a couple of people in an office that you talk to when you want to find out about courses and some computer screens to tell you schedules and locations. Ah, you say, schedules; there must be some kind of time there after all. Well, we do one thing after another, just like you do, but we still don't have time like you do. There's screens flush against the walls here, all over, and there's, like, announcements on them. Like Mrs. Swartz's Conversational Spanish is about to start in room twenty-five or Lenny's Advanced Programming in room twelve. The teachers also send out thoughts to their signed-up students by looking at a list and projecting the idea. That usually works, but just in case you're being, like, a bit absent-minded there's these screens all over. Same with performances and stuff; music students love to perform and there's little concerts all over the music department: anything from *Bebop Classics* to *Stephen Foster recitals, Mozart Trios* and *Deep Grunge Deviance.* I wrote those down so I'd remember. My dulcimer guy plays with this folk group, with like mandolins and guitars and fiddles. They call themselves *Apparently Appalachia.* And there's some dead rock band guys doing guitar and drums stuff. People do serious shit like Math and Philosophy too, but not me. Not yet. Maybe I'll do some American Literature soon; always wanted to check that out. I mean it's my country after all. Or it was. Is it still? Most kids around here are from the States, whether they're like, Oriental, Latino, Middle Eastern, African or some European thing. I say that 'cause I can't tell them apart. Not really. I can fake it for conversation 'cause they all speak English, but they all got their accents and attitudes, maybe only half or a quarter American, if you know what I mean. Some of them are still Iranian or Venezuelan or Polish or Japanese, with just kind of a little layer of American on top, like icing.

Whereas me, I'm American, maybe not all American, but for

sure an American in Heaven. Question is, when Americans get to Heaven are they Americans or Heavens? I figure I'm about halfway between. I still look at stuff like an American, but I'm losin' it fast. With a Granny like mine, who, like, questioned everything about society and politics and stuff, I never did have that *live free or die* thing. My dad was some kind of sixties rebel but you could never get him to spout it, and he was never the kind to have a flag out front like some of our neighbors. Only thing I can recall him getting excited over was that Oliver North thing and I was only a little kid at the time. Not even that, really – the eighties, I was a baby then. He must have brought it up once in a while later when I was about seven or so, 'cause I can still see Mom at the dinner table telling him about somebody called the Sandinistas and hubris, and me not knowing what either word meant. One time years later at some special dinner, maybe Thanksgiving, he did say he thought Reagan's policy in Central America to be appalling. Granny chipped in something about how he could have been a textbook fascist, if only Nancy hadn't gone through with the lobotomy. That's Granny for you; more outrageous than any punker I'd ever met. I got Eric to play her some Dead Kennedys: *Holiday In Cambodia* or some shit. She thought they were great and asked if they did any fundraisers. Shoulda played her *Too Drunk to Fuck*, that would have been a laugh.

I bet you're wondering about her second husband, my granddad. The first you've heard about. Well, she unloaded him years before. There's all that crazy gambler talk, and I guess it's at least partly true, but I bet she drove him crazy with endless politics and pissing away almost as much of his winnings as he did, and then divorced him, got half or whatever, got my dad through college and stuff, snagged this little cottage near the Cape on some land her friend Peggy inherited, and just went on with her life like he'd never happened. He, that's William Thomas Gifford to you, found some Georgia gal when he was vacationing in Hilton Head, (someone who loved to play dress up and throw dinner parties according to Granny), married her and moved to Atlanta.

We went for Christmas once. It was pretty good for us kids, we got spoilt big time, Lucinda made sure of that – for what reason I'm not sure, maybe to impress Granny back on the Cape – but there was some kind of falling out while we were in bed and we never went back. I tried to squeeze the dirt out of Dad a few times, but he wasn't talkin'. I'll bet it was political though.

Which kinda brings me back to the Americans or Heavens thing; seems like you just kinda get distanced from it all: the stuff that you thought was your life and your country. All that America the Beautiful and saving the world for democracy stuff, it doesn't seem to matter much any more, least not to me – I guess it could to some. I mean I'm pretty sociable with my peers, always was, but I can't say I've met everybody. And I guess those soldiers from Iraq might still be feeling pretty strong on that kind of thing. Discussed it with this French chick who died during her first year at some tiny college in New Mexico – fell while drunk believe it or not. She said she was starting to feel the same, that all that France-is-best stuff sounded stupid now. But she did still really miss her brother, who she'd been really close to since her mother... well she didn't wanna talk about that.

You know that stages of dying thing? The denial, anger, bargaining, acceptance thing? Well it's kinda like that. There's definitely the denial stage; I see it everywhere. Only just out of it myself really. People won't face their death. Some won't talk about it, others act like it never happened, you know, go on just the same; others talk like they're gonna go back soon, like they're just waiting for their tickets to come through, like they're on a long holiday, away for the winter instead of just two weeks. And it's not hard to do, with Happydeadland here being so beautiful and fun. There's not many in the anger stage, but I meet a few, and I can see others are like on the edge of it. They're through with the party stage and are realizing that marriage and career and status shit just ain't gonna happen for them. There just ain't no lawyers or stockbrokers, generals or CEO's here. And a few are asking their guides about going back. Can they swap bodies with someone? Yeah, if you can find someone there who wants out badly, and that usually means an attempted suicide or serious downer shit of some kind, and therefore a fucked-up life to walk into. How about another life altogether then? Yeah; rebirth is do-able, but are you ready to, like, not be Jay or Genna any more but be a fetus and then a baby and then a little kid, and maybe not well-off and white? This is like just what I've heard in conversation various places; I haven't approached Sonja on any of this. I notice car crash victims like me are prone to this *gotta go back* thing. Not me though; like it here too much.

Do I see much bargaining going on? Well, it's kinda part of the anger thing. People talk about deals they try to cut with their guides, like if I do this can I have that?

Guides usually can't do the magic acts they're asked, although a lot of what they do do seems like magic to newbies, and I think that's how it comes about. Acceptance is what I'm coming into now. I've had my fill of rebelling and whining and am ready to settle down, although what to do I'm not sure. Just what I'm doing now I guess, and maybe a bit more as time goes along. I know: no time, but you know what I mean. Sonja said once there's lots of babies to either work with or adopt, but I think Eric and a couple of those girls off the Island will be enough for now. You know I'm really committed to Eric; just can't leave that boy behind; wanna be there for him as often as I can. Maybe all this is just one more example of how life here is not that much different from life there.

So after the ladies coffee klatch I climbed aboard my magic chariot and charged off to Andrea's. Stupid really, it was middle of the day there and she must've been at work. I resisted the womanly impulse to snoop about the place in search of her elusive charm – like what's she got that I don't – and floated out the window and roamed the streets for a bit. That's still a lot of fun for me, zooming about in and out of stuff like some kind of mad bird. Maybe I'll grow out of it one day and be all mature and wise like Sonja, but right now having fun is more fun than being wise.

I thought about my loser brothers for about five seconds and felt like *No thanks, not today* – not ever maybe. We'll see. What would they care anyway? They never gave a shit before. Sibling rivalry you'll be thinking. Yeah, and so what? Look around you; see it in your own family? Sonja told me once it's fine not to like certain people, 'cause being honest helps you get to who you really are, but that nurturing it kinda makes you sick, especially here where emotions are, like, the stuff of life. I think what she really meant was *Get over it, Mel,* but she's too well-mannered for that kinda talk. Good old Sonja; she's been a great help to me. Maybe I'll go see her someday. Right now she usually just pops by to see me. And she's got this uncanny sense of when to show up. Like always a good time, never a bad one. She says that's what being a good guide is all about: knowing when to show up and when to stay away.

Maybe I'll learn that one day. Maybe if I hang with those chicks on the Island more I'll figure it out for myself. Now there's a good project to get started on.

21. Pastor Liz

Went to one of Liz's things in church: she was good, really into it – great talk, almost believed her myself. In our family, sermons were, like, frowned upon. Even Granny wasn't allowed to give them, and she was usually hot for stuff like that. This is at the dinner table, right, the only place we really, like, gathered together, and Mom really ruled the roost there. *Politics has ruined this country worse than the civil war ever did, and I'm not having it ruin this family*. That was her line pretty much. Anyway, I'm talking about Liz, and boy she really tore into that sermon. Later she told me it was just Episcopalian-lite with an evangelical edge since she'd seen Jesus for herself at that big open air thing I told you about. Maybe I'm easily impressed, or need some of that old-fashioned religion, but she sure was convincing to me – close to tears I was, I really was. When I told her that, she said that although she's had to adjust her theology a bit since dying, her faith has never been stronger, and she feels no need to apologize for putting it out there so passionately.

Personally, I wondered about the need for passion now that we're in Heaven, safe and well as you could ever hope to be, but I didn't want to say that exactly. Everyone's different and everyone has different needs. Maybe that sounds a little too wise for a lass like me, but I've come a long way since dying. And besides, I've always wanted to be a lass and it looked like the only way it was going to happen was if I used the word myself. I thought about bribing someone, Sonja maybe, but it seemed like, you know, stupid, so I didn't.

I'd heard Christians talk about their passion for Jesus before and wondered what they meant, especially if they were women. With Liz, I think she meant, you know, enthusiasm, fresh enthusiasm – like she now had more certainty than faith, having seen Him, or someone doing a very good impersonation. That's a topic around the student lounges from time to time; are these Jesus sightings the real thing, some mass hallucination, or some stand-in from central casting? In a way it's a bit like all that debate on earth about the Elvis sightings, and I don't mean that to sound disrespectful, but it is. And that's interesting coming from me – I used to go out of my way to sound disrespectful. I used to think just about everything was a crock. But I'm all grown up now and I know that only *some* of it is a crock.

But just to let you know, I guess, that there's still plenty of opinions about what's going on here. It's not like arguments disappear once the life after death one is resolved. Heck, getting through that is just like getting through a door to all these other debates. Even Liz says she thinks more seriously about Mohammed and Buddha now that she's here. We took a walk after her service and really got into some good stuff. Maybe because I acted like I was really interested, which I was, in the way she communicated her points, like she mentioned the bible from time to time, but not enough as to put me off. She talked more about her personal feeling for Jesus and what he was all about – like you walk with Jesus on your way to God. He shows you the way and helps you when you get lost from time to time. And I guess that's not too different from what I heard on earth, maybe it's just hearing it personally from someone who cares that makes a difference.

Eric agreed with that when I told him later. First of all he thought it was interesting that I'd met up with a minister – me of all people, who, according to him, went out of her way to trade insults with every vaguely religious person at school. Well, he's about half right: I didn't favor any religion; I figured they were all stupid and people just followed them 'cause they were too scared to think for themselves. At least three guys called me an existentialist for saying stuff like that and when I got mad one said *No, no Mel, that's a compliment*. Eric still laughs about that, which reminds me of how he's still so much like his old self. I know I've said that before, and I see him in kind of unusual circumstances, when he's out of body at night (everyone else sees him as a tragedyboy in a wheelchair who struggles through every day), watching him laugh remembering schoolstuff like that he's just like the old Eric – the walking, running, dancing Eric. Not that he danced much. The odd party, he didn't like clubs – hated the music and what he called the competitive sexual vibe. But me, I surfed through all of that, loved it. Not because I was that sexy or competitive but because I could see through it all and laugh.

I see Eric so regularly at night (his night not mine; we don't really have that here) that I'm keeping him up with all the news, just like I would on earth. So he knows all the latest about Dad and Andrea and the icky brothers – Ick and Yuck I call them. He was never too fond of them himself, nor they of him – called him Becky behind his back 'cause he's wasn't, like, guy enough for them. Didn't do that guy stuff, never did. Course that's one reason why I liked him so much: no testosterone tantrums.

Telling you about the Jesus debates back there reminds me: some guys say they've met up with people who claim to be aliens, like not from earth. Trouble is – because you can, like, mold your body to your desires here, and most everyone wants to be, like 27 willowslim and gorgeous – these alien claimants look just as human as us. Grant told me the one he met said he was from, where now? umm, the Plediades? No, I think it was Pliades, and he'd heard about another one from Sirius, from Ali I think. The debates are like, intense, because they look and act like us, more or less, so they could be just, like, attention seekers or your basic bullshit artists. Grant asked him all sorts of questions about his home planet and the answers sounded, like, genuine, but later he thought maybe they could have been made up. The guy told him he was here in the spirit world of earth, to get acclimatized before being born. That kind of threw him, as it would a lot of guys here, 'cause a lot of people come here, like, not only not believing in an afterlife but also not in reincarnation at all. So, although a bunch of folk are like really hot to go back, somehow, anyhow, a whole lot more think it's complete bullshit. So, there you go, more stuff to argue about here.

Not that I argued much with Liz, not at all really. We got a nice vibe going. She doesn't come on all righteous and I don't ratchet up the teen rebel lingo. So with these fly-by visits from Jesus and lord knows who else (prophets from other religions I mean), where does that leave big-time believers like her? *Well,* she says, *obviously there's Heavens and Heavens.* Something she'd kinda always figured on, what with that St. Paul thing about suddenly being caught up into the third heaven and seeing stuff he couldn't, like, talk about.

So little folk like you and me live on one of the regular heavens and Jesus and all the important religious people live on another?

Well, kinda sorta, she said, *but it probably wasn't that simple.* But obviously growing in spirit got you places. That made sense, at least to me. Those guys in that other place that Sonja took me to – the gamblers and all that – they sure looked like they had some growing to do, although I'll admit it, I didn't think much about it at the time. Just being there was weird enough.

But I'll have to admit, if there's Heavens and Heavens, like Liz thinks – and I'd have to say that Sonja's dropped a few hints in that general direction – I'd be kinda interested in checking them out. I guess there'd be like different societies and races and religions and what not, and maybe they'd be just as weird to me as I would be to them.

Let's face it, weird's no judge of anything. People, especially my kind of people, say it all the time, and after a while it gets kinda meaningless, but we go on saying it anyway. Like, *Wow that's weird,* or, *How totally weird.* Maybe it's like our generation's version of *nice,* as in *isn't that nice,* or *how nice for you,* or *have a nice day.* I think everyone knows it's dumb, but some natural laziness keeps us from being more inventive. Maybe it's just a teen thing, though most of us are in our early twenties. Hard to keep track, with no real days or weeks, or calendars that make any sense, but plenty seem to know somehow. Of course you get some clingers that want to be just the age they were when they came here. I've seen a few *still nineteen* t-shirts, usually on the kind of people who'd wear *No Surrender* back on earth. Yeah, you guessed it; attitude still reigns supreme. For some it's all they've got, even here.

22. Something Different

Here's something different. I know, you've heard enough different stuff to last you a lifetime already, but here's something really different: Sonja brought him by a while back. Like if I was on earth still I'd say last night, but I'm not and we don't, so not so long ago Sonja came by while I was just kinda lounging around my room. Actually I was wondering whether I should maybe get my nails done, which is weird for me as I haven't really cared about that kinda stuff since earth, actually way before I came here. I was flippin' though this design book, and it's amazing how many they have in there. So intricate – makes the ones on earth look sick.

Sonja's got this guy Jeff with her, quite the looker too – more manly than I'm used to around here. Teen testosterone isn't manly, though they all seem to think it is. I wondered if she was maybe trying to set me up with him. Maybe she thinks my thing with Eric is sick or something – my dalliance, she once called it; had to look it up before I called her on it. Which I did – full bore. Eric a dalliance? Uh, no-oo. Anyway, she really wants me to hear all about Jeff's life here, 'cause it's well, different.

See Jeff was a dope dealer on earth. Called himself a consignment shipper – middleman guy – hydroponic pot, high grade grow-op shit mainly, some ecstasy – from Canada down to California or Oregon. Started out as an independent operator, till the heavies moved in and forced him to defend himself. *Me with a gun,* he said, *I never would've believed it. Canadians don't pack pieces. Not in the national psyche.* Especially in B.C., where he was from.

Had to take lessons; didn't know about bullets or nothin'. Usually just showing you were packing was enough to, like, get you respect, but his luck, or something like it, ran out, and a little shootout in the woods and he was dead. Spent a couple of what was probably years, ghost hunting his killers down, trying to screw 'em up whatever way he could. Picked up a few tricks on the way, like how to focus your desire into a sharp thrust of energy so it actually affects the physical world – make doors thump, and glass fall and smash, turn on taps and cause floods. Really screwed up their clubhouse, which was built like a fortress; made it so they wanted to burn the place down themselves. They even got some kind of African guy who lifts curses to come into the place and do his stuff, but Jeff just stood back and watched some funny colors swirl about that were supposed to make him scared and run away. Then they up and sold the place and moved away. Course he just followed them and tortured them some more. Eventually the fun wears thin and he sees vengeance has become his life. Then he realizes he's not just a loser but a dead loser, which sounds way worse. He's laughing as he tells me this. See, he's not like nasty by nature; it's just the way his business evolved – he had to become a shark to survive.

So he kinda pulls back to see what else there is. Well, as a lot of us found out, if nothing else there's flying, so he starts on that – the Pacific Coast Highway became his favorite. Up and down the length of it, hugging all the curves at high speed – what a blast that was! Then it was out over the water to Hawaii and around that part of the world. Maui had this great vibe, so he just stayed. Found a bunch of dead surfers and hung with them. I think you can see where this is going. When he said he met up with someone who offered to really show him around I said, *Knew it! Knew it! It was a guide right?*

Sure enough he gets to the real afterlife and finds out how totally cool it is – really digs that for a while, meets up with some buddies and his one grandparent and uncle who've passed, gets shown all the stuff I've told you about – or most of it. Figures what he really wants to do is go around and kind of inject good vibes into crappy situations. Uses that same focusing thing he'd done to screw people up. I said *that's for angels isn't it?*

No, we can do it too, he says. *All you need is the right attitude and a few tips from an old pro.* He said he'd, like, nose out trouble wherever, and just inject a dose of good vibes, like topping up a coffee with cream. And finding the cups of coffee was no problem; people were always arguing and fighting somewhere; it never seemed to take long. When I say fighting, I mean personal stuff, not wars. A mister good vibes angel, Jeff was. And he got to just love it: spreading those loving vibes about. It was like the more he did it, the better he felt. Getting folk to kiss and make up through what he called 'liberal doses of love' really blasted him. This love shit was really incredible, he remembers thinking, better than any drug he ever tried. I thought oh-ho, a lecture about going clean. But he said no, no lecture, just what happened to him. Did I want to check it out? He could take me for a spin. Sounded like a date so I went for it.

Sonja said she had something else to do and disappeared. Jeff and I change levels almost immediately and were back on earth in no time, buzzing around some city streets. Doesn't really matter where, I guess – somewhere. I just kinda hung back and did what I was told. We found this man and woman arguing – foreign language but we could feel the vibe no problem. I think the guy had been drinking. I dunno, he just kinda looked like it. The woman just seemed pissed: maybe he'd been screwing around, maybe he'd wasted her money. Typical domestic, Jeff says, kinda grinning. I'm thinking it's funny he'd use cop-talk when this beam of orangey light comes out of his chest and, like, surrounds the couple like smoke. We wait and watch. It kind of settles on them, like dust would if there were no wind. They both seem to slow down and not shout so much as talk. There's a couple more mini eruptions and then they suddenly rush together and hug. Tell ya the truth, it was all a bit gooey Disney for me. Maybe I'm conflict junkie, but I couldn't believe it somehow, like Jeff had played some Harry Potter trick on me.

But he denied it, and said he was just real good at figuring where he'd be the most help.

Then he took me somewhere else. It was still on earth, least as far as I could tell, then we walked through a wall and I knew for sure. He seemed to know his way around so I guessed he'd been there before. Big old house: mansion I guess – corridors and rooms everywhere – a lotta art on the walls, mostly boring old crap – gloomy shadowy stuff. Like why anyone would have that on their walls is beyond me. I follow Jeff and we wind up in a bedroom, well bedroom and sitting room in one – lots of space and fancy furniture. Old fashioned fancy – some easy chairs by a window looking on to a garden. I'm trying to guess why we're there when a woman appears from nowhere and sits down – well, slumps down – depressed looking, wearing an Oriental slinky housecoat that I really admire.

She looks to me like a spoilt rich bitch, all screwed up about shit that don't really matter, but what do I know, so young and inexperienced and dead? Jeff does another beam of light thing, goldy flecks in with the orangey stuff. It surrounds her but it's like it can't get in somehow, like she's got some kind of invisible wall about her. *Yeah,* Jeff says, *sorrow and self-pity, I've been working on her for awhile.* He doesn't say how he got to know of her, so I make a point to ask him later. I see now she's got a set of works in her hand and is getting ready to syringe it. I've known a few kids go that way – bad news all round. You can't beat smack. Best you can do is maintain with methadone, and some say methadone is worse – all addiction and no high, like gambling without any winnings, ever. Ultimate sucker trip. Jeff's pretty little clouds sort of disappear into her, or just kind of melt away. She's like smiling as she lifts her left foot for the needle, and afterwards she's got that blissed out junkie look as she nods.

We leave her to her bliss, Jeff grinning like he's accomplished something. He says *No, no achievement there, just wanted to show you a toughie. She's so wrapped up in herself she can't hardly ever see out.*

I remembered some book from school called *The Prison of Self,* but not enough to really say anything intelligent about it, so I just, like, nod and look like I'm agreeing. I probably am but know that Jeff's kinda got me in a knot – the cute knot. Damn, I wasn't really ready for that. He's that kind of serious cute that I could get really stupid about, even here where I'm so dead and wise and all.

Next we're in some kind of boardroom, corporate HQ maybe – suits around a table, two chick suits as well. Excuse me but they're all suits. I'm told there was a time when putting a bra inside a suit was considered a turning point in human affairs. Gees, feminism musta been some kinda religion back then. How else could they have fallen for that? Suits are the armor of power; whoever's in them gets caught in the trap. By my generation, if you want to call those late-nineties, know-nothings a generation, we'd seen the light. The bullshit of suits corrupts absolutely. That's Eric's of course; didn't know one chick in school that wanted to do the suit thing, even the lawyer wannabes. Seen too many Michael Moore movies probably.

So I'm watching the scene, waiting to see what Jeff's got going here. I figure this isn't his first visit and that he's got most everyone in the room sized up already. Never sat in on one of these before and only have TV to go by. Actually it kinda looks like TV – the expressions, the waving of pens and opening and closing of folders, the wishing that so-and-so would drop dead. One chick's got the neckline the other's got the legs. Funny really: six guys, all looking serious and not at the chicks. Maybe it's marketing or something. Jeff lets go this stream of golden light that begins to swirl around the conference table. Maybe they're bankers or something. It's hard to imagine them getting it on or otherwise having some get-down fun. You know, singing Barry Manilow songs at the neighborhood karaoke and chugging back their whisky sours. Soon they're all kind of swathed in this golden smoky light. Jeff says nothing to me. I think I'm supposed to guess the game plan. I'm having trouble getting past square one: what kind of lift can you give sourpuss sharks like these? And who'd want to anyway? Well, Jeff would I guess.

I get an answer to my first question with telepathy from Jeff: what you give to sharks like these is love, the kind of love that has no conditions attached. You give it to them and see what they do with it. Sounds like playing with a basket of kittens, I think. Yeah, Jeff replies, in telepathy that is, that's about it. Well what if they don't do anything, just kind of suck it all in? Sure it's a crap shoot every time, but there's no squandering resources here, 'cause you can't waste what's always there. Anytime now, I think, he's gonna come on like some preacher dude with this pipeline to Jesus thing. Call it what you want, he replies, make it generic if you'd prefer – a link to love. I know I'm supposed to think this is cool, and I guess I do, but then there's these sharks in suits drinking down all this love and not doing anything with it, like fixing third world hunger. Jeff says, *Hey, let's focus on being kind to each other at lunch first.* That gets a laugh and I think I see his point.

After we move on he's got this line about action without desired results and how it's neat to just give. He says the love is like an electric current and having it pass through you is just such a hit that nothing else matters. He makes it sound like high grade coke. He says it's not a bad analogy but totally without the come down later. Well, thinks I, you can't beat that.

Just one more cool thing about the afterlife, I suppose. The list is getting longer, I know, and maybe you're getting a bit tired of it all being so wonderful and all. I probably would if I was in your place. Jeff must sound, like, unbelievably hot. Well, hate to brag, but he is. But wait till you hear the next bit. Jeff takes me to this, well, bedroom really. Somebody's bedroom. You can imagine what I'm thinking, but I don't get any time to think it, 'cause a guy and a girl are kinda sitting there, looking not too happy, like they'd had a falling out moments before we got there. Jeff tells me he's been before, been working on them for a while, injecting love into their situation. Okay I get it, more of the same now? He nods and goes into his thing, and they're surrounded by a lovely rosy light, which slowly kind of melts away into them. Only difference I can see is that they begin to talk a bit. Still kinda glum but exchanging you know? I recognize the stage: been there, done that. Usually it's a good sign; you're on your way to a truce at least, if not a full tilt forgiveness session. Then I get this thought from Jeff: *Tune into my mind and I'll show you the back story.*

Back story? That's like the background stuff for people in a movie, right?

He goes, *Yeah, except this is their life. Was their life.*

Okay, so I try to tune into his thoughts – not easy.

You're trying too hard, he says. *Ignore them for the moment and focus on me. Close your eyes.*

So I do, and it seems to work, somehow. Later Jeff calls it a mind-merge. That's good enough I guess. I see the two of them driving somewhere. You know, staring straight ahead like there was something they didn't wanna see. They park and get out. Walking somewhere, not holding hands, but then they are. It's like a movie this and it's somehow Jeff's memory. He hears me and says I was working with them then, tailing them like a private detective. I know this must be significant but I can't think how. So they walk into this building, kind of a strip mall unit, but a little fancier than most, some nice trees outside and stuff. And there's some people standing around at the front that they have to walk through. Looks a bit tense. Then we're inside; it looks and feels like a doctor's office. Oh shit, now I get it: she's in there for an abortion. Not what I wanna think about right now, thank you. So, of course, the guy's there alone while she goes in. Then Jeff fasts forward a bit. She's sleeping and he's sitting watching. I also see Jeff in the corner looking on sadly. Well maybe not sadly, more sympathetically. He's in his own mind movie, I'm thinking kinda wowed, forgetting for the moment that I'm in there with him, somehow.

Then there's another fast forward and we're in another room with the two of them, still kinda sad looking, both of them, but not quite so sad. Time heals I guess. I know it did with me. But there's something strange here; bits of the room keep fading at the edges, like someone's rubbing them out. But the whole space seems, like, much nicer than before – bigger, and more luxurious somehow, even if it does keep fading at the edges. I'm working on that one when Jeff whispers, though it's a telepathic whisper, that they're dead. Oh yeah, right, why didn't I think of that? Loaded up on some really good smack and nodded out without knowing it, he tells me. Think they're still alive in their same room when actually they're dead and buried. So Jeff's just trying to bring a little love into their lives. Cool I can dig that. He asks where I got that hipster talk. I laugh. If it was a hundred years ago I'd bat my eyelashes too, but it's not and I'm not sure I can anyway. Tried it in front of mirrors a hundred times and got the giggles every time.

Jeff doesn't seem at all impressed with either my charm or my wit, and we, like almost instantly, are in some bar beside some argument quickly heating up. Jeff says, in response to my first though, that no, he didn't know this was about to happen, but that in this place it's usually a good bet that it's about to. He has us stand back a bit. The guys around the table are arguing about something – sports, politics, religion, who knows, they're past the point where details might tell you and into the macho bitch stuff. Sure they're wasted too: beer buttheads. There's some other guys watching, like real interested. Don't know why; it's all such bullshit. Jeff flashes some really bright white light at them and they all jump back or disappear and then reappear. It all happens so quick I can't really tell. Then he tries a softer, creamier version of the same light for the guys at the table. I watch it settle on them as they shout red-faced. The whole thing seems to peak and then fall apart, like they've run out of steam. Soon they're ordering another round and laughing, although it still looks like a powder keg to me. Jeff leans in and says, *Yeah they could go off any minute, but it's a challenge to see just how long I can put it off.* It was all kind of icky and I wanted to get away, so we did. I didn't wanna seem ungrateful, but Jeff was okay with it. Said they were really just another version of the suits around the table really, but the challenge was the same wherever you went.

I asked if we could go back to his place. Kinda forward I know, but I just couldn't wait any longer. Surprise, surprise; said he didn't have a place, just kinda grooved around – a gypsy, an astral gypsy. *There's lots of us,* he says, *we're just hard to pick out.* So I ask him to show me where he likes to hang out when he's off duty. Suddenly we're in the mountains – some mountains, well they all look the same to me – probably the Rockies, but who knows. We're way up high on a ledge, overlooking not just a valley but a range of peaks and valleys in between. What can I say? It's like way beyond breathtaking and into some whole other thing. We stayed there for ages, just relaxing and comparing notes. Eventually I can't resist it and kiss him. Wow, what a vibe – it's electric. Within seconds I felt like opening my legs a mile wide, but Jeff has other ideas – figures. Hottest guy I've ever met, and we're like, on a mountaintop, and he wants to stop and show me something. Later, I said.

Later (that's when the steam comin' outta my ears kinda subsides), it turns out he's got this thing where we sit cross legged and stare into each other's eyes while projecting love from our hearts. Yeah the same kinda love as before, except between two people. The eye thing is a strain, as his are so beautiful, but as we work on it, whatever *it* is, I do begin to feel a tingle right there in the chest area, which for a girl, ain't no surprise. Then it really starts to get, like, heavy. Big tingle all over, like the build up to an orgasm but an all-body one instead of down in the swamp there. Jeff says it's called the heart chakra orgasm. I said call it what you want it's pretty darn sweet.

Course I ruin it all by telling him about Eric. How I can say anything up there in all that incredible beauty is crazy enough, but Jeff was cool; he like really understood. Didn't have any sweetheart on earth himself, but had met plenty here who did and suffered for it. Told me a few stories then we went back to my hood and he said goodbye-for-now kinda thing. I gave a big hug and said I wanted to see him again real soon. He said sure and was away. I turned and tried not to cry – almost succeeded.

23. More of The Same

That's just a chapter title really, but it's how I feel when I go back to the family. I mean, stuff happens and I guess you wanna know since I brought you up to speed in the first place. Well, first off, Mom and Dad have sat down and discussed me, without tears and anger and stuff. I know 'cause I was there. Dad started it, talking about how he feels me around from time to time. He was like trying to convince Mom, but she says she felt it too and talks about that time in the store in front of the yogurt, and suddenly they're sharing in a way I hadn't ever seen, least not since I came here. Not hugging and weeping, thank God, I wasn't in the mood for that, more holding hands and talking quietly and intently.

After a bit they get on to Ick and Yuck and I lose interest. Well not instantly, but quickly. Yuck's case is still way off, but the bail's no problem and a lawyer with serious debts to Dad has been hired. Sounds like they're believing his bullshit story, Yuck's that is, you know the usual I-had-no-idea-she-was-nine-told-me-she-was-eighteen stuff. I can't believe Dad would go for this crap, maybe he's just trying to ease Mom's mind. Sonja said I should go easy on him, like my anger would somehow get through to him and upset him. I wasn't in the mood to hear that. For some reason I blurted out that he had a ways to go before he was finished so why should I ease his way with love and forgiveness? Sonja agreed with the ways-to-go bit, which shocked me as I wasn't too sure myself and having Sonja say it kinda made it, like, irreversibly true somehow. But she figured any love I could spare would, like, lighten his load somehow, maybe even stop him from doing worse. *You never know*, she said, *love's funny like that, you just never know how it's gonna affect people*. She didn't say anything about Jeff, but I was thinking about him and what he does. I think about Jeff a lot, probably too much, and probably more about him than what he does. I might be in love, but we'll get to that later. So I'm thinking, in between romantic bits, can I do a Jeff, am I up to it? The answer is maybe but not with Yuck – somebody else maybe, but not him.

So I tell her that, straight up. She tells me she understands and we leave it at that. I keep remembering that thing about you always hurt the ones you love, but it doesn't make sense 'cause I can't recall a time when I ever loved him. He was a total shit from day one, which for me was about three years old. He probably spat in my baby bottle when Mom wasn't lookin'. Right, I've got no proof, but it'd be right up his alley that kind of action – jealous little prick.

Now onto Andrea; hadn't been by one of her meditation sessions for a bit, just kinda wrapped up in my own stuff I guess. Went by one afternoon, hoping my aim was true, you know, and shit it was. She was just getting cross-legged when I got there. We had our usual little chat and she was just as cool as always. I told her as much and she said she was happy living her life one day at a time now. She's just not as anxiety ridden as most people she says and isn't really sure why. Sure yoga and meditation help, but she knows a bunch of women who do the same and are still in knots about men and clothes and careers. Having her parents die and leave her the condo all paid off certainly didn't hurt, of course. She's straight up about that, which I appreciate. I've known too many whining princesses with daddy's credit card and car who could do the patho-sicko thing the minute any speck of shit would hit the fan. Sometimes she wonders what's keeping her going, 'cause she doesn't have that anxiety-status-aging crap going like so many people she knows. Says she doesn't really worry about anything, which I more or less believe. I mean she seemed that way when I was alive on earth. She was so cool I remember wondering if it was an act, but it wasn't, then or now. Tells me she takes courses just to keep herself amused; started yoga just last week; fits with the meditation real well. She asks about my life and I bring her all up to date on that. She kinda nods when I mention the Jeff thing, like she sees my dilemma right off. That's girl talk for you I guess. She doesn't say much but I can tell what she's thinking – that I'm headed straight for trouble. I know but I don't want to know. Maybe I can juggle. Me? Sure I can juggle, but Eric's my blood brother, we been through a lot together. Look at what we're going through now. Maybe it's like me going to Europe for college, or him maybe, and planning to like, keep in touch and be as tight as the distance will let us, but just not being able to pull it off. I mean, if that was what was happening, it'd be tough but we'd live through it and always be, like, tight. I know we would, 'cause we been through it already. But people change, I guess, and he could as he grows older. And that's something he's gonna do while I, like, maybe not stay the same, but sure don't grow older. That's the weird thing about being here; you do change but not like you do on earth. I've talked it over with Sonja so many times, but it's so hard to, like, get it across. It's like one of those discussions which go on and on and never end. Sometimes you think it's because of earth people get married and start families and get mortgages and go all serious, whereas here we just keep having fun. Course there's the family shit like I told you and the whining about being dead and all, but once people get past that they have a blast, while back on earth the family-career-mortgage thing lasts for ever and ever and people never seem to get happy again – not really happy anyway.

You're right: I'm tying myself in knots here. Sonja tells me people still get married here, but not to have babies, though you can still adopt and if you get a little one it winds up being the same really. A baby's a baby, right? So enough knot tying. What got me into this anyway? Talking about how cool Andrea is. Well, she's sure got her shit together far as I can tell, and doesn't seem like overly concerned about splitting with dad. I think she can sense how much it would screw up Mom if they stayed together. Course that just means Dad'll meet someone else a year or two from now and it'll be the same thing all over. Maybe Andrea just doesn't want it – the inevitable break-up – to be her fault. Or maybe that's what I want her to want. Okay enough.

After that I visited with Eric. Got there kinda early. He was reading and checking his fave sites. I sat and waited like before. I don't mind; he's worth it. When he finally got into bed and fell asleep and we made contact it was lovely, both of us feeling very affectionate and caring. So sweet and nice I don't really wanna talk about it if you don't mind – too private. And no; I didn't mention Jeff. How could I, after that? Get real. Being upfront is one thing, but picking the right time is like way more important. People need to be in the right mood. Eric must've been in the right mood, 'cause he fessed up about Cara, who's kinda taken an interest these last few days. She started by asking if she could sit with him at lunch, not that he doesn't have his own set of buds, but he was by himself that day for some reason (oh yeah, Rick and Brad had an track meet) and it just kinda went from there. Third day, she's telling him that it's not just pity, that she's always admired him from afar but thought she wasn't good enough or smart enough. That I can see. Cara always, since grade five at least, had this low self-esteem thing going. I'd always figured it for an act – a way to get people to feel sorry for you even if they didn't like you – which is kinda where I was with her, though I didn't really dislike her, just didn't care one way or the other.

So Eric's not really convinced, but he's enjoying the attention and the company. She walks him home and pushes his chair if he'll let her. He says sometimes he feels more like she needs a big furry dog than a guy. Course I'm jealous as shit and ask if they're sleeping together yet. He looks shocked and says *no of course not*; he's not one to rush into things. He glares at me and says, *You of all people should know that*. And I do, but I just kinda blurted it out. So I ask if he's looking for my blessing, which I guess doesn't sound too, like, friendly, and he says No, he's just telling me and why is this getting so weird? I say I dunno, maybe 'cause he's bringing someone else into the picture. He says it's easy for us here, like, not in the world, to talk like this, but there, during the days, when he's strapped in and below everyone like he is, it's a different story. When he's awake he only remembers tiny bits and pieces of our time together here, and never tells anyone 'cause he knows they'd think he was cracked. Then he throws his arms about me and whispers *It's hard Mel, it's really hard.*

I know Eric, I know, I say, feeling so many mixed emotions that a recount will probably be necessary.

So we go through all this and I can't tell if I'm trying not to mention Jeff, lying by omission, or just being polite and waiting my turn. Anyway, I never do mention him and we kinda heal up that other stuff about Cara, mainly because I insist on them being friends and whatever else they want 'cause Eric really needs someone – other than his mom that is – to look after him down there. He doesn't agree, of course, guys can do everything by themselves don't ya know, but he relents, or I stop talking about it, one or the other or a bit of both, who cares really, and then we make love like nothing's happened. And then, in case you need reminding, he slips back into the sleeping body thing and I'm outta there.

So that just about covers it, I guess, the ones on earth, the important ones, the ones I worry about and maybe feel responsible for. You do, you know; you feel responsible for their mental health, even if you say to yourself or your dead friends here, *I don't give a shit; that's their problem.* You can't do that *I never asked to be born* stuff again. Some kids try it on, but it's like so unconvincing. Those that took the cancer/meningitis route are prime it's-not-my-fault candidates, but because things are such a blast here you don't get it often. For most of us, our dumb shit stupidity caused their grieving, and although the length of their grieving is like, their thing, you got it going and keep feeling that you can do something, or do several somethings, to wrap it up so's they can be done with it. Some kids get really outta shape over this very issue and just wanna end it all, except that you can't do that here, and besides, it would just be a boring rerun of the first time anyway. Kinda funny when you think about it – actually came up with some chick I was sitting with in the lounge. Didn't know her at all, don't think I'd even noticed her before, and that's exactly what she said, *sometimes I just wanna end it all*, and we looked at each other, saw the craziness of what she'd said and let go with the chick screech. That's something you never forget, no matter how long you're dead. Other stuff, yeah, but those precious items, like rebel yells and pussy power and all that charm school shit, that never leaves you – too useful.

Just thought of something I didn't mention before and should have, so you see just how much we sweat and debate over this stuff. We have discussion groups here, like more than just sitting around the lounges shooting the shit, although we do that often enough. There's organized discussion groups, in certain rooms, just like classes really, except there's no tests and papers and shit. One's called *Who Dies and Who Doesn't?* Another's *Death Is Birth Is Death*. And there's another one I walked past one day, thought it sounded cool, but didn't have time to join in and forgot to go back and now can't recall the name. Well, no one's perfect, not even us dead people.

24. What It All Means

About a week or so has gone by since I last wrote – going by Dad's paper anyway. I've been thinking over all this stuff and wondering if maybe I should tie it all together somehow. And when you get onto that kinda stuff, you slide helplessly into all that meaning-of-life shit. And here that obviously becomes meaning of life and death and everything else, which is quite a package. Pastor Liz and I had a chat about all that.

I figured she'd have something intelligent to say, so I dropped in for a visit. She was happy to see me but warned me that it was all stuff she was still working on, that she had no final answers for anyone. But I said that was okay; I just wanted to know what she was thinking on it now. I wouldn't hold her on it. I mean everyone's entitled to change their mind. God I do all the time, about every ten minutes or so.

Liz figured that her outlook was still pretty much Christian, even though it's obvious to her that other religions get their believers here too. She thinks that loving your neighbor and trying to know God more and more deeply as you go is where it's at. For her the spirit of Christ is about the brotherhood of all men and that means all Buddhists and Muslims and atheists as well. It's not about forcing Christianity down their throats; it's about embracing them with the love of Christ no matter what they believe. But she believed that on earth already. Now she knows the truth of eternal life instead of just believing in it, which is great, but what can she do for those on earth? It looks as though they still have to struggle with their faith in the face of all the suffering and injustice in the world. I tell her about my project, well she knows kinda, but not the bit about how it's gonna get down to earth. That's Sonja's specialty. Least she was the one who let me know the various options and problems. *Well,* Liz says, *that's Spiritualism then; at least that's what they called it when I was alive*. She's not so sure about mediums. There was always aspersion cast upon it in the Christian community. Aspersion I had to think about for a minute. Maybe it wasn't all justified, but she always wondered how the mediums knew what they were getting was truthful and accurate. Were they testing the spirits to see if they were of God? I said I didn't know about that, but wasn't I of God? Wasn't I telling the truth as I knew it? She said, Yes, I was, but how would the person I was giving the information to know? I said it was gonna be Eric and we were so tight there was stuff I could say to him that he would know could only be me. I was gonna lay my hand on his and have him write. It was called automatic writing and Sonja said people had been doing it for a coupla hundred years – with varying degrees of success of course.

Liz asked if I could trust myself to give out the truth about the meaning of it all. Was I experienced enough to be speaking on such lofty matters? Probably not, but I knew what I knew and was ready to talk. People could judge for themselves – they usually did anyway. I felt she was testing me, to see if I really believed in myself. Suddenly I thought she didn't have faith in herself but was covering up by passing the ball to me. But I said something about why only the experienced should speak out; shouldn't the young have a voice too? and she seemed to agree. Again, like she was testing me.

After that I went by Eric's, like I do most nights on earth, and when he came out of his body and saw me, asked him how he'd feel if I tried some automatic writing through him. I was surprised, he hadn't heard of it before. I explained how it was supposed to happen and then he knew. He wanted to know if he had to be hypnotized, or just go into a trance. I didn't think so, but I said I'd ask Sonja and get back to him. I thought we should just set aside a time every day, say eight in the evening – his evening.

He wasn't sure that he'd remember. He barely remembered

anything of our times together as it was. It was fine when he fell asleep and emerged, then everything was just fine; it was like we'd never been apart, like nothing ever ended – like eternity. But then he had to get up and be alive and forget it all – or almost it all. I said maybe if we practiced every day his memories would get bigger and better. Maybe he could put it on the net, he said, looking brighter. His father had already offered him the start-up money for his own web site, but he'd deposited it while he worked out all his crippleboy issues. That could be the theme: something that wouldn't get people just feeling sorry for him, with all that politically correct good will. *Okay,* he said, *let's go with the eight pm thing. If I'm busy just crack the whip,* I laughed. Trying to get Eric's attention when he was into something was impossible when I was alive. How was I gonna do it as a ghost? Maybe Sonja could give me a couple of tips.

That first night I really made an effort to get down there on time, which can be hard from here. I kept checking in every once in a while to see what he was up to: home from school, glass of juice, Cara phones, he feeds the fish, talks to his mom, helps with the veggies for supper, checks his email. Course his room's on the ground floor now so's he can get around easy, but you'd probably figured that out yourself. I had just finished a music class myself and was practicing a new song. Really enjoying myself actually, so much so, I was afraid I'd miss our date. Finally he finishes supper and retires to his room. Don't you just love that, retiring to your room? Don't even need a pension. Watching, I can see his parents aren't so worried about him anymore, which is good, and not just for me and my guilt. He boots up and stares at the screen. It's nearly eight on his bedside clock (a really cool melting Dali item from Paris I think, when his parents were there).

He sits and stares some more. Okay I try to tune into his thoughts like Sonja said. It's not that hard. He's thinking about what he's forgotten. He knows there's something but what is it? That's where I come in. Talk to Mel, I think, in the middle of his thoughts, between one and the next. He feels it, I know he does, but is puzzled. I think it again, hoping the light bulb will flash on. *Let me give you thoughts, let me give you words,* is what I think next. I'm sure I can feel a response. Something like *Okay then.* I see he's got a file open, so I think/say some stuff about the accident. Just after, when I was in the ambulance with him. He kind of gets it, but I can feel him thinking, *Nah, it's me imagining what Mel might have been through, no one'll believe it.* So I think, who cares, just do it anyway.

So he lets me go on for a few lines before he feels a rush of embarrassed stupidity and shuts down the file. Sonja had warned me to expect this and said I'd be lucky if he didn't just delete the whole thing, but he saves it and titles it *Mel Remembers,* which is funny as the whole exercise is about him remembering. So I leave him be. He's got a life too, not to mention homework and a bath to take. I'll see him later.

Course I'm thrilled with success, even a little, and want to see what Jeff's reaction is – pretty cool as it turns out. Not sure why; maybe it's just not his thing. We go off for a while, injecting happiness and merriment into some down-and-out situations. He says to me, *It's so now and so high energy, isn't it?* Well, who could disagree, it is. Amazing, the effect you can have on people if you really try. We make love again but we're not quite so connected as before, and we don't even try the other thing. I come back to my room, not quite sure what went wrong then I go to the lounge to forget my troubles. Someone suggests dancing and off we go.

I lose myself in that for a while: lotta new people I haven't seen before, some cool tunes – Just what I need. See Grant dancing with a chick I don't know, wait till they're losing interest, catch him while he's sipping on a tall one. Seems pleased to see me. Me too, he's neat guy. Get him over to a quiet spot and tell him about my new project. Well, basically the thing about What It All Means and how he sees that. He laughs. Haven't we done that to death already, like ten times over? Yeah, sure we have, but

I wanna put his opinion in the book. Look I have my little recorder thing here. Shit it's small, can't get used to that – about iPod size I guess. They didn't have them when I was on earth but I see loads of kids with them when I do my flying around.

He wants to take a walk – says he can think better, so we go outside the club. Like everywhere else here, it has these beautiful surroundings – gardens and shit, you know? Like the classiest of neighborhoods. Some kids complain that it's just too nice. You know, too tidy, too perfect. I can see their point but it doesn't bug me as much. Some of them are like dead graffiti types and use their new found powers to paint the place up. But them someone else can come along and erase it just as fast. Yeah, rivalries develop, sure, but it's not my scene so I don't pay much attention. So we stroll on a bit and Grant says suddenly that it's all too much for him. Maybe he just has to be here longer, he doesn't know, but being ten times more alive than when you were supposed to be alive, he still can't get around that. Says he feels like superman most of the time. Then he flies straight up, hundreds of feet, just like that, does a somersault or two and zips back down again. I grin. *I mean,* he says, *you spend all your life worrying about dying and then this? I mean, how weird is that? Why aren't we told? It's like the biggest conspiracy to keep us in the dark and deal us crap. My parents thought it was all over once you died; told me to make the most of all my opportunities, and gave me all the support a guy could ask for. Now I'm here, with more opportunity than they could ever imagine gathered in one place and I gotta go back and see them depressed 'cause they think I'm no more. I mean, it sucks. Big time. I'm not one of those kids who are, like, thrilled to be free from the family trap; we had a great house, my dad took me golfing since I was, like, twelve, and all I had to do was mow the lawn and clean the pool. Fuck, I had it made. They wanted me to go into law, despite my not-too-great marks, but you know, they never pushed like some parents. Dad said, Hey take a coupla years and bum around, I did. Be a ski bum in Aspen, bartend. And now they think it's all wasted. And there's nothing I can do to change that. I mean, how fucked up is that? What does it all mean? I don't know but I wish I did.*

I sympathized with Grant, I mean really, and told him so. He asked if what he said was kinda what I was looking for and I said sure. Just then a buddy of his appeared and they were off on some adventure. That male bonding shtick, that's another thing that goes on here like nothing's happened. Ah well, so what, says I. I start thinking about Kurt and what he might have to say about the meaning of it all. Following Sonja's much repeated advice, I think about him real hard and express the wish to be with him, not like some teeny thing where you wish you could date a rock star, dead or alive, but like more determined. Then I'm in a new place – somewheres – like a forest, or a some bush somewhere: big trees but not tangled undergrowth; you can still walk. I'm thinking what's Kurt doing here, communing with nature maybe, when I come across a cabin, a log cabin, like from the Wild West days. You ever see that old Redford film *Jeremiah Johnson*? Like the one he lived in, toward the end, where just about everything that could go wrong has gone wrong. It wasn't like a biggie Redford flick so you might have missed it. Anyway, like that. I've been here a while, as you know, but I'm still wondering *why this? Why now? Why me?* stuff when I see Kurt sitting on a stool – a three legged, wooden stool that I once seen someone use to milk a cow, or was it a goat? Some school trip way back when. He looks up and smiles, like he's glad to have a visitor. I tell him about my project and ask if he'd like to add a few words. He says sure. For him it's what you want you get. Maybe it takes a while, but you get it. But you gotta see that other stuff comes along with what you want, like it never comes by itself – it's always got buddies, buddies you may not like. He got what he wanted, more than once, but he didn't care for its buddies.

It seems like a weird way of seeing What It All Means, but it's his ideas I want not mine. There's questions I'm dying to ask him – you can probably guess what – but I bite my lip and let him talk. He goes on about how he could say a lot of other stuff – philosophical stuff about the meaning of life, especially life back there – but he can't help but think that wanting and getting sums it all up. Sure a lot of wanting is subconscious and surprises you when it happens. Trick is to be aware of what you secretly want. Then when it happens you're at least half-ready for it.

I finally have enough courage to ask a question. Is this what he tells the kids he visits at nighttime on earth? Well sometimes he gets to that, but mostly he talks to them about depression and suicide and that stuff. See, a lot of them are like copycatting him. He feels responsible for their choices, although he knows he isn't. How many of them would do it anyway, whether or not he'd set the example? Hard to tell, but he's betting more than a few: understandable too, when you see their family situation – pretty fucked-up. Who's he to tell them what to do? He doesn't, but he does tell them what to expect when they get here, and not just the nice stuff, the shitty places too, 'cause a lot of them will wind up there, just like he did at first.

We stop recording, or whatever this little thing does, and he asks about Eric and I can kind of fill him in on that. He nods like he approves. I'm not so star struck that I need his approval but it's cool to see it anyway. I want to ask about his life but kinda feel like I'm intruding. Maybe sensing my reluctance, he says he's still kind of a star here and he has to be careful about his appearances. He much rather be a nobody now, but that's one of the buddies that fame brings – it just doesn't end nicely when you've had enough. Course it's only dead young people that know him, but there's enough of them around to keep him here in the forest. He's not exactly a hermit but he does keep to himself a lot. And yeah, he still plays guitar and writes songs, mostly on acoustic. He feels more gentle here. Thinking about putting together a folky-type band sometime, but there's no rush. He's been to a few concerts by other rock bands, just to see what it's like here. He disguises himself with a beard and curly black hair. There's some great energy here, a happy energy, but it's just not the same: not demented enough - that crazy, don't-give-a-fuck energy. For some reason I suddenly think of Mom talking about the joy of throwing caution to the winds, which I think she did maybe three times in her whole life. I don't mention it though. Neither do I bring up U2 or the dance clubs I hang out at – probably not his scene, but the island for murdered girls seems like something he'd like to know about, so I tell him all about it.

After leaving him to his privacy I wondered if maybe I'd kinda said too much and threatened someone else's privacy. Couldn't decide really. You try your best and fuck up anyway. So where else do I go but back to the island? Course that's what it's like here; you think too much or too strong about someone or someplace and you're there in less than seconds. So I'm standing at the edge of the water like I'm ready to cross, and I think, *Is this really what I want to do*? Well, the girls here have as much right to a say as anyone else, even if they are young, dumb and inexperienced. Okay dumb, I said it. Course I'd never say that to their faces, but I would've on earth. How come I've changed? Little Miss Mercy and Compassion, that's me. I'll bet there's an outfit to go with that – kind of an Audrey Hepburn meets Florence Nightingale thing. Just kidding! All those poor dead girls – starved, beaten, mutilated – it's just so terrible, but here they are, just like me, without a bruise or a blemish. Okay, psychic bruises for sure. And look at those dead soldier boys. All the kings horses and all the king's men couldn't put Humpty Dumpty back together again, but the afterlife can put anyone back together, just like that.

Lisa, I found in her room no problem, reading a fashion magazine, no less, and almost up to date. She had her usual scared bunny look that always brings out the mom in me and she seemed real pleased to see me. She passes her time doing next to nothing but seems pretty happy with it. After the kind of life she had on earth I guess anything, even the boring repetitive routine she has here, is better. She asked if we could go see a movie again sometime, and I said *Sure, wanna go now?* Then she said, maybe not now but sometime soon maybe. I think she liked the idea of going more than actually doing it. What I call the ice-cream-that-never-arrives syndrome. I'm more of a let's-eat-right-now sort myself, as I dare say you've figured by now. We chatted about this and that and when I got bored I told her about my little project: What It All Means. She said something about just not knowing about things like that and I thought, yeah, that's about where she's at, and quickly changed the subject.

Suze, I couldn't track down. No one seemed to know where she was – probably walking around in the woods by herself, according to a couple of random chickoids. So off I went, clueless pretty much, wandering around hoping, just like I would have on earth, never for a second remembering that I could just think hard about her and be there with her. It's that adjustment thing; life here seems so like life on earth in a lot of ways that you keep forgetting that actually it's way different. So there I am, a dopey little red riding hood clumping about when I hear this voice from somewhere. *Did ye ever wanna piss on someone from a great height?* Yup, there's Suze way up in a tree grinning down at me. I don't know whether to laugh or be insulted, so I call her bluff by floating up to right beside her and spitting playfully in her hair – doesn't fizz on her at all. She says, *That's nothin', I knew some chicks who killed a homeless girl and then pissed on her.*

Fuck Suze, says I, *This shit don't impress me, I bin downtown.*

Okay then, she says. *Let's do lunch. I know a lovely little hideaway on the coast highway.* Then I laugh. Basically 'cause she sounds so – I dunno – LA cool.

I tell her – that's after we're back down on the ground, like normal people, although there's no such thing as normal here – that there's some cool spots to do lunch where I live. Suddenly she's reluctant, like the island is her hood and she can't step outside, but I convince her to hold my hand and whoosh, we're there, by that neat little storefront café that I described being built before – wrought iron chairs and tiny circular table tops and a few trendoids looking very cool. I get us some lattes and cheesy fries. It's so great to, like, pig out on fatty shit that you'd never have dared on earth. *Watch that waistline girl* don't mean shit here.

Suze seems seriously impressed, like someone who's outta their depth but is loving every minute. I could actually see her get interested in some guy here, if he was cute enough, before she was like, you know, too lean and mean for love. Course I don't say anything about that, but I tell her about my little tape thingee here and my What It All Means project. Suddenly she's like all mouth. She leans towards me and lets go. Back when she was so-called alive she thought it all meant nothing; it was pointless, stupid, a waste. Every time you got a half-inch ahead you got dumped on. Everyone was out for themselves, looking to rip you any chance they got. You always had to be, like, your own guard dog and keep him hungry so he'd be, like, always alert to danger. She reminded me of how I felt about my so-called brothers, but I got beyond that with almost everyone else. Anyway, she went on like that for a while, describing her life in hell, at least that's how I saw it, and saying, like, how could there be a God? Why would he allow it – such screwed-up people and screwed-up lives? What was the point of all that? It was, like, a total waste. Drugs, sex and violence? The only fun part was getting high, and even then you always had to watch for someone stealing your stash, if you even had one to steal. So when she died it was with, like relief more than anything. Like, *Thank god that's over,* although she couldn't see how there could be a God. How could he create so many shitty stupid people? So anyway, it was like *Thank god that's over, now what?* And then the *now what* part turned into a real fun adventure pretty quick, what with all the people she met – all the dead people. So then she thought even if there's like, no God, there was at least fun, big time fun, and some of it clean – downright wholesome even. We laughed when she said that – big screechy chick laughs. Okay, so not much meaning but plenty of fun. So maybe fun was what it all meant. Why not? It made more sense than religion and wars and money, didn't it? I said, *Hey Suze, sounds good to me.* And I meant it in a way. It was just her opinion, but still, all that grown up adult sensible stuff never made much sense to me. Why weren't houses free? Why did people have to work so's not to starve? But that's like one of those thoughts too hard to think so nobody thinks them. I remember saying it to Dad once, and he said, *Slow down there girl, you're gonna wind up back in the sixties thinking revolution for the hell of it, and you ain't gonna like where that lands you.* It sticks in my mind 'cause he, like, never used the word ain't.

So after some more yack and lattes and laughs, Suze figures it's time to head back. Like she's gonna get caught if she doesn't sneak back in before dark or something. But it's like Sonja told me early on, people bring their issues with them and you gotta deal with them like they're real.

After Suze, I'm thinking of that book I read in grade ten, *Catcher in the Rye*. Okay, I know, every kid reads it and thinks it's like the most meaningful book ever written – for a few weeks anyway. *Perennial favorite,* Dad called it when he saw me devouring it a second time. But that guy, I mean the writer, not Holden, must have some thoughts on What It All Means, I'll ask him. Course I can't remember his name, so I think of Sonja, I'm there, and she's not busy like she sometimes is, and I ask her. She says, Yeah she knows the guy but he's not here yet. By that she means dead; he's not dead yet. I'm thinking he must be like, ninety-five or something when she says, *Well, we can try visiting during his sleep time and see if he's out and about*. So we do that. Sonja knows his name, Salinger, so we have no trouble finding him. It's just like here; if you're ghosts, like us that is, you just think hard about who you want and you're there. Turns out he lives not that far from where I grew up. Not that that matters, he could be in California or China and we could still get there in a flash.

So we hang about the bedroom and wait above a sleeping body under blankets. I know it's, like, an invasion of privacy, but we don't mean any harm, and it's like the only way to, you know, catch him on his way by, 'cause some people do leave their body every night and go places. And if you don't catch them as they're exiting, as Sonja puts it, they're gone till morning. I asked why we couldn't use the think-of-them method when they're out floating around. She says that although they're, like, officially out of body, they may well not be conscious of it and wouldn't respond. It's like they take their sleep with them as they go about parts of the spirit world. Sounds weird I know, but it happens a lot she says. Or they'll respond, but dopey like they're half asleep and dreaming, or they'll be the type to stay firmly anchored, as Sonja says, like totally in sync with their sleeping bodies. The only way to find out what type they are is to hang around at falling asleep time and see what happens.

I get kind of excited at the prospect of putting his words of wisdom into this, like they'll be wiser than mine and everyone else's. I'm already, and probably have been for a bit, at the stage of not being so impressed with his book as I was when I read it, of thinking that I've matured beyond that stuff, but I'm not even sure about that. Anyway, we wait and wait but nothing much happens. He turns on his side and that kinda stuff but never emerges. Eventually Sonja says I think we're outta luck and I pretty much agree. Oh well, you win some lose some. We get back to Sonja's place and put our feet up. Sonja wants to know how I'm doing and stuff. I fill her in on all the things you've heard about recently. She sounds kinda impressed. *Am I doin' good?* I ask, grinning.

You're doin' good, she says. We laugh like nothing really matters after all. As if What It All Means is just a way of passing the time – this non-existent time we have here.

We start joking around so much I almost forget to ask Sonja

for her take on the deal. Not that I haven't heard most of it at some time or another. There's that time thing again – can't get away from it. She tries to sum it all up (she really did say I'll try to sum it all up) by like insisting that life really does go on forever, there is no end, in sight or out of it (she really said that too) and it's all about growth, in both mind and heart, so that you're kinder and more loving as you get smarter and wiser. *Sounds good to me*, I said and we laughed again. I mean, it sounds great don't it, even if you can't see any way you're going to get there.

Sonja was impressed with my attempt and I was impressed that she was impressed. I always liked being teacher's pet. She said, *What about Eric?* While she was going on about how invaluable it would be, I was thinking shit why didn't I think of that? A chick ownership thing I guess. Anyway, I get down there pretty much at the right time, which is a surprise as I wasn't really thinking of it. He's in front of the computer – a blank screen – looking ready and waiting. Course I can't ask him his version of What It All Means. We're just starting out, have to keep it simple; anyways I can do that when he's asleep and out and about.

I try to focus in on him and put thoughts across: simple stuff like *Eric I'm here and happy to be here* and *Hope you're good tonight*. He types some. I look closer. It says *Hope you're happy* and *Maybe it'll be good today*. His shoulders are hunched and I know he's tense and probably frustrated. I wish he would relax. I push the thought *Relax!* at him. He types the words: *I'm so refreshed from relaxing*. Shit, we're getting worse instead of better. Then he types a question: *How do you relax there?* Suddenly excited, I focus. He types: *dancing, swimming, flying*. Hey that's pretty close, although to be accurate, flying here is more exciting than relaxing. I guess I was thinking recreation in general. All fired up now, he types again: *Sounds like big time fun*. I focus: *Sure as hell is, Doctor Spock*. I say that 'cause it was an old joke between us. I said it once when we were outrageously stoned and we never forgot it. It was like a flag planted in the terra incognita of stonedness. Terra incognita was Eric's phrase. Anyway, he types it out word for word. *Yipee!* But I could feel right away he was, like, thinking he'd made it up because it was one of our things. *Shit!*

That, more or less, brought things to a standstill. He closed the file and sat there, staring. I tried to influence his gloomy mood but it wasn't happening, so I left, knowing that a couple of hours would have to pass before he'd be thinking about bed and all. I went back to my room and practiced my dulcimer lessons. The beautiful sounds of the strings kinda chilled me out and in a while I was back to some kind of Mel normal. Sonja had warned me about taking in too much of Eric's 'stuff' and I think I'd done it that time – his frustration, his doubt and maybe despair. I didn't want to use that word despair, maybe 'cause I couldn't stand the idea of him feeling that. Doubt I was ready for. Despair was scary somehow, like it was something you couldn't defeat, even with all that Happydeadland stuff at your disposal. Anyways, I defeated my own defeat with music, which made me kinda, well, proud or something – at least for a minute or two.

Then I knew it was about time for Eric to be sleeping. He was lying there in the dark (his dark; it doesn't look that dark to me, kinda twilight-ish and glowing, if you know what I mean). I had some earth time to fritter away while I waited for his eyes to close and the out of body thing to happen, so I let my mind wander a bit. I found myself thinking: *walls, doors and windows; doing the house thing*. Was that What It All Means for people on earth? I made a note to make a note. With me, the good ideas usually get lost before they get used. Next thing I know he's out of it and then out of his body, sitting there looking at me with a little grin, like, oh yeah, here we are again. I hugged him right away. It felt good. He described his frustration and doubt at the message thing and how it had depressed him. I said, *Hey you don't look depressed now.*

And he said, *Yeah, it's weird isn't it. It's like I'm one person when*

I'm Eric awake during the day and another when I'm Eric asleep at night. When I'm here with you life awake seems so, like, narrow and dim and simple. So how much did I actually get right before? Anything?

I said, *Not too bad for beginners, not completely accurate but, like, pretty close.*

That seemed to cheer him up. He said he'd try to remember when he woke up, but shit, it was so hard when you were there to keep your, like, knowledge alive. There it was like whispers and rumors, vague echoes of dreams. Here and there, not enough to keep you thinking about them and connecting them up, just enough to disturb any kind of coolness you may have put together for that day. I sympathized as I usually did, although I was starting to wonder if it was all fake. Like, could I really *feel* what he was going through? Or just say I did? 'Cause once you get adjusted to this world – this whole being-dead-and-not-coming-back thing – and start to have fun you kinda lose interest in all the crap you used to think was, like, so important. But I forced myself to 'cause I like felt I owed it to Eric and my folks: like playing the dutiful daughter and the loyal friend, and really thinking it's real, but slowly seeing it's, maybe not fake exactly but full of the wrong kind of stuff.

So to get out of that one I tell him about What It All Means and ask him for a contribution. He realizes almost right away the weirdness of it. He's giving me his opinions now and I'm like recording them, but later he'll be taking it all down with automatic writing or automatic keyboard entry. We laugh about that and really can't believe it'll all actually happen. *Maybe you'll get bored*, I say. *Maybe Cara will think it weird, or your parents*. No, his parents are so supportive; they'd never try to shut him down on any project. I can believe that, I know them. Or I used to know them back when I was alive.

So he's like ready to go, as if I'd warned him a week ago and he'd been taking notes. Firstly, he figures that *shit happens and you deal with it*. Course I know that one; he's been pushing it for years, long before the accident, but now he wants to expand on it. *Like how*, I say.

Like shit comes in different varieties.

No kidding, I say, laughing. Like before shit was always bad shit, like trouble, like a hassle, like a total pain. Now shit is just anything, anything that happens, 'cause he's seen, right down there at wheelchair level, where you're with the little kids who, like, don't have to buy the adult package – the society bullshit – that things just happen. Pens fall out of reach, you lose your pin number, a leaf falls from a tree, Green Day write a song, your cell stops working, Cara's got a cold, history sucks, you get rained on waiting for a ride, but hey – dinner's really good, Mom's been to the gym and is buzzin' with endorphins, Dad shares his bonus like candy. You know, there's these endless waves of things happening and you just kind of learn to surf the ripples. I say that sounds like a cool way to live life, but is it really What It All Means? Then he throws me. No, Eric's always been smart, way smarter than me, but not like a nerd. People who never really knew him said he was nerdy, but they just hadn't seen his kinda cool. He's one of these guys who when people look back on their youth, like, realize he was the coolest dude going but were just too fogged up with macho bullshit and trendoid dorkiness to see it. Anyway, he's been taking a philosophy class since the accident and I think that's where he got this gem from. He says to me, *You can't separate meaning from the activity of life. It's not apart it's inherent.* Course he's smiling as he says this, so I just sorta kick him like I used to and he just sorta chuckles. *Yeah*, he says; it's something the teacher said, more or less, but he really, like, agrees with it. Like, don't I see how beautiful it is? Before I get a chance to answer, or even think of an answer, he says, *Truth is beauty and beauty truth*. So naturally I kick him again.

Anyway, that more or less sums it up. We had some private time after that, stuff you don't need to know about, and then he felt that urge – that weird kind of tiredness that wasn't really tiredness – to rejoin the sleeping body. *Here I go,* he said as a goodbye. I returned to my room and kinda unpacked my baggage. Leaving Eric was always tough. I couldn't escape the feeling that I'd abandoned him. Even though he had a life, a good family and a woman who seemed to care deeply for him, although Cara had always seemed the flaky type to me, I always felt I could and should be doing more. But what could that more be?

I slept on it. We don't really sleep much here. Well, you do when you first arrive, but it's more like a habit than really being wiped and eventually you realize it. But you still can take naps and stuff, like just lying back and chilling out. When I'd had enough and was getting itchy I had a shower and dressed. Checking myself out in the mirror I decided I didn't like what I saw and figured a visit to the retro-mania clothing store was in order. There's a bunch of great stores here, something for every kind of taste and style, and mine is mix-and-match retro. And the great part is it's all free! Just like everything else here – no money, no debt, no sweat. What could be better than that, I ask you.

25. What About Andrea?

What about Andrea? I thought later. How could I forget her? If I was still on earth and had gotten to know her like I know her now, she'd be a role model for sure. Exceptionally cool. So after a couple of tries I get there at the right time. There she is, meditating and the other Andrea appearing like magic. We sit, ever so nice and normal, on her couch, opposite her meditating self, and I share my What It All Means project with her. She's interested and wants to contribute, which is good 'cause I'm at the stage of getting obsessed. Can't think of anything else sometimes. I thought she might wanna hear the others but, no, she's happy to dive in. She thinks it's all about finding out who you really are. It's a long trek because everyone puts labels on you and you believe them. You think and act as though you were the label you've been given. First off it's the baby thing; there's not much you can do about that, but the other family ones, which come at all angles from every member, you can wrestle with them as you get older and more confident. Then there's the religious and society ones; they all wanna tag you and treat you accordingly. Eventually, you're just a walking bag of tag reactions. Your behavior and your life is controlled by what others think of you. You can't remember who you actually are. *Before I got my act together with meditation,* she tells me, *I was so caught up in being the rebellious daughter, the wayward wife, the feminist outlaw and half a dozen other ego traps, I thought the roles were the actor.*

Okay I get it, I think, but where are you at with it all now?

Now I'm Andrea the director: the director who writes her own script, and stars in her own production.

And that's What It All Means?

That's what most of it means, maybe not all, probably not all. I mean there's all this God stuff isn't there?

You bet.